Ellen slipped her fingers down inside the collar of Armand's shirt, enjoying the touch of his unseen skin, imagining the rest of him, all warm and strong and smooth . . .

His breath hissed through his teeth. "That's taking unfair advantage. Remind me never to buy a stick shift again!" Throwing the car into the next gear, he freed his right hand and slid it up the length of her leg, his fingers caressing the warm flesh of her thigh through her silk skirt.

Ellen giggled. "Stop that! I feel like a teenager on her first date!"

"Good, then let's ditch your friends and go park somewhere. We can make out in the back seat."

"This car doesn't have a back seat!" She laughed, her head spinning with the delicious promise of his touch."

"Then we'll go to the park and I'll throw my jacket on the ground and pull you down beside me and we'll make sweet, endless love."

Ellen closed her eyes and drew a shallow, trembling breath. She began counting to ten to get hold of herself, but she'd only gotten to two when his voice sent fresh waves of desire washing over her.

"Ellen, don't you want me as much as I want you?"

"Oh, Armand, that's like asking Cinderella if she'd like to dance with the Prince!"

WHAT ARE *LOVESWEPT* ROMANCES?

They are stories of true romance and touching emotion. We believe those two very important ingredients are constants in our highly sensual and very believable stories in the *LOVESWEPT* line. Our goal is to give you, the reader, stories of consistently high quality that may sometimes make you laugh, sometimes make you cry, but are always fresh and creative and contain many delightful surprises within their pages.

Most romance fans read an enormous number of books. Those they truly love, they keep. Others may be traded with friends and soon forgotten. We hope that each *LOVESWEPT* romance will be a treasure—a "keeper." We will always try to publish

LOVE STORIES YOU'LL NEVER FORGET
BY AUTHORS YOU'LL ALWAYS REMEMBER

The Editors

LOVESWEPT® • 141

Adrienne Staff and Sally Goldenbaum
Crescendo

BANTAM BOOKS
TORONTO • NEW YORK • LONDON • SYDNEY • AUCKLAND

CRESCENDO
A Bantam Book / May 1986

ISBN 0-553-21759-3

Published simultaneously in the United States and Canada

PRINTED IN THE UNITED STATES OF AMERICA

O   0 9 8 7 6 5 4 3 2 1

One

Crash!

There went Dan's Garfield mug, its cat image smashed into a million pieces on the hardwood floor.

"Oops, sorry Garfield," Ellen Farrell grumbled aloud as she wobbled beneath the ungainly weight of a heavily loaded cardboard box. She kicked the scattered ceramic shards out of her way with one foot.

"Young doctors have no right to have so many *things*," she muttered, sliding the box from her bent arms onto the floor with a thud. "It's ridiculous." She squashed an empty box of Cadbury chocolates with the toe of her tennis shoe. "Dumb! Stuff all over the place. All over *my* place!"

Without pausing for old emotions to set in, Ellen rushed back to the bedroom and returned carrying scuffed hiking boots, a baseball cap, and a six-pack of imported beer.

Pushing a handful of chestnut hair back behind one ear, Ellen took a minute to survey the cluttered doorway. A shiny brown suitcase, its sides bulging from her frantic packing efforts, leaned drunkenly against the umbrella stand. Next to it was the cardboard box stuffed with medical journals, papers, dog-eared Travis McGee mysteries, and one slipper. A pair of men's boots poked forlornly over the top.

"Okay, we're almost done." She stuck her hands into the pockets of her jeans and took a deep breath, then shook her head slowly from side to side. "No. Correction: We *are* done. We've been done for a long time, Dan Newlin."

A month ago she had nudged the young doctor right out the door. It was over, finished. Being lonely was better than pretending, wasn't it? Yes, it was, her stubborn self insisted . . . but it still hurt. She and Dan had been seeing each other for over three years. During that time he had become so much a part of her life that it had been especially painful when Ellen finally realized their relationship was going nowhere.

Working longer hours at the hospital had helped; at least she had the other nurses to talk to and could avoid the chilling stillness of her apartment. But it wasn't enough. It wasn't what she had dreamed her life would be. There was a time when she had wished Dan would be a permanent part of her life. She felt the hot sting of tears behind her lids and pressed her hands to her face. She felt tired, weighted down by some unnameable sadness.

As she moved back toward the tiny bedroom,

Ellen wearily lifted the heavy fall of hair off her shoulders and let it drop back in a dark chestnut wave. Her clear gaze fell on a man's razor standing in a cup on her dresser.

"Damn!" Her eyes flashed as she stared at it. Was it possible to hate a razor? she wondered.

There it sat, dull and lifeless, with a few dried hairs clinging to the edge. It was a perfect reminder of what her relationship with Dan Newlin had turned into: Ellen, loving and giving, and Dan, clinging and ready to take. When he was an intern, Dan had claimed the excuse of his hectic schedule. But then his internship had ended, and nothing had changed. Where had the feeling gone? The pleasure in being together? Either it had all ended a long time ago, or she had only imagined it in the first place.

Well, it was time to cut her losses. She had called Dan and asked him to come over one last time to collect his belongings. Afterward, she would be free to move ahead with her life.

She grabbed the razor and, with the perfect aim of a Harlem Globetrotter, tossed it neatly into the nearest wastebasket. Then she marched back into the living room, pulled the apartment door open wide, and pushed and pulled and dragged every last thing out into the hallway. There, done! *Finis*, as they said! She smiled, brushing her hands together in front of her, but her smile wobbled, then slipped away.

Trembling, Ellen leaned one shoulder against the doorframe. She was shaken by a sudden feeling of panic. Tears sprang to her eyes. What if this were all she'd ever know of love? What if this were all the fates had in store for her? No passion, no wild, breath-snatching romance, no magic.

Her lips trembled, and a pain as sharp as a blow hit her in the stomach. Eyes closed, she held on to the door for one dizzying moment. When . . . *when* was she ever going to get lucky?

But then she straightened her shoulders and pulled her heart back up out of her tennis shoes. Oh, no! She was not going to give up so easily. *Something* was waiting for her. *Someone*. And if it was taking a little longer than she had hoped, well, love would be just that much better when it finally arrived!

The ringing of the telephone jarred her thoughts, and she shut the door quickly on the last remnants of Dan Newlin as she rushed to answer it.

"Hello? Oh, Laurie, hi!" Laurie Westin's voice always brought a smile to Ellen's face. After three years of marriage to Rick Westin and with a baby due in a couple of months, her best friend still sparkled with a fresh, vital, honeymoon happiness that never failed to touch Ellen.

"Ellen, listen, Rick just brought home a fellow from the new jazz group playing in town and—"

"And you would be eternally grateful if I'd come for dinner and bring dessert," Ellen teased, knowing what was coming next.

"Oh, Ellen, hush. Rick says he's a great guy and we'd love you to meet him. You need to get out, Ellen. And besides, I'd love to see you," Laurie pleaded softly.

Ellen laughed huskily. "Laurie Westin, will you never give up?"

"Of course I won't. You're responsible for my

meeting Rick and I won't rest until I've returned the favor! So come, please?"

Ellen slipped down on the couch beside the phone. "Laurie, I don't mean to seem ungrateful, but do you recall Rick's last friend! Remember— the flutist? I was six inches taller than he in my stocking feet, and he kept kissing my chin. No more musicians! I'll take a raincheck and come tomorrow night, just me and some chocolate chocolate chip ice cream! That I know I can handle. Thanks anyway, Laurie; today is for cleaning house and getting rid of the cobwebs. . . ."

And suddenly, as she placed the receiver back in the cradle, Ellen knew just the way to sweep out those cobwebs.

Minutes later, a loose-fitting sweater flung over her shoulders, she scrambled down the last flight of stairs to the lobby.

"Clarence," she called to the middle-aged door-man standing near the front desk, "when Dan Newlin comes to pick up the last of his things, please tell him everything but his Garfield coffee mug is outside my apartment. The mug met an untimely demise too terrible to talk about!"

Clarence grinned his instant approval. "And you, Ms. Farrell? You goin' out?"

"Yep, Clarence. Out . . . and away."

She stepped through the door just as a black alley cat, all ribs and tail, darted across the side-walk in her direction.

"Oh, no! Shoo! Don't you cross *my* path," Ellen scolded, not moving one inch. She'd had enough bad luck to last her a lifetime. "Scat, cat!"

The cat turned tail and ran, and with a smile Ellen hurried down the street, hopped into the front seat of her car, and drove off into the early morning sunlight.

Rolling down the windows, she let the breeze lift her hair like a flag, the cool, autumn-smelling air washing over her deliciously. As the pavement sped by, all reason, thought, and sense were caught by the cool breeze and tossed happily into the lovely blue sky.

At the next stoplight she turned the little car to the left, a turn so sharp and polished, it made her smile. And as the fates would have it, as she barreled down Wisconsin Avenue, Ellen Farrell began to turn her life around.

It felt good just to be moving, to watch the landscape sweep by and feel the rush of air on her face. She was a bird set free, wings full and ready for the blustery fall breezes. She felt wonderful!

Turning onto the interstate, Ellen speeded up and flipped on the radio. A popular rock tune filled the car, the music pounding with fierce energy. Ellen hummed along, one foot on the gas pedal, the other tapping in time to the music. She put on her sunglasses and rolled the window way down. The broken white line flashed and disappeared beneath her tires. Then, like a bottle of soda pop that's been shaken and suddenly opened, all her emotions fizzed to the surface. With a quick glance around she drew a deep breath and screamed.

Loud. Long.

It felt fine!

So fine, she tried it again, ignoring a low-slung sports car passing her in the left lane. Another good loud scream, and the weight that had been pressing relentlessly against her chest for months vanished. Her heart felt whole again. She saw the autumn reds of the leaves of the trees bordering the highway, and the white clouds scudding across the blue sky. She looked at it all with wonder, feeling like a prisoner freed from jail, a patient released back into the world. Cured. Well. Happy. Oh, she'd make it! So what if love wasn't easy? Who ever said it was going to be easy? She gulped a huge lungful of autumn air, grinned, and gunned the engine, feeling better than she had in a long, long time.

She was doing eighty-five miles per hour as she went by the low-slung sports car that had passed her earlier. She tossed a carefree grin at the driver. Then she did a quick double-take, her eyes opening wide behind her dark lenses. The driver was gorgeous! Sexier than his sports car, and she'd always lusted after that particular make . . . of car.

One arm resting on the window, his shirt-sleeve rolled to the elbow, Armand Dante had watched the rapid approach of the old Mercury in his side mirror. A frown marred his handsome face. Maniac drivers! he thought, one dark brow rising in disapproval.

He caught a glimpse of flying hair as dark as a brushstroke of burnt umber against the blue sky, and a pair of huge sunglasses. He turned, aiming a cool, reproving glance at the reckless young woman, and got knocked right into tomorrow by her smile.

For a second he thought his heart had stopped beating, but then he felt it racing along nicely beneath his ribs. His lips curved in a faint smile, and he pushed the sports car to eighty miles per hour.

Ellen felt slightly dazed. She slowed, flicked on her turn signal, and pulled into the right lane. Counting to ten, she kept her eyes on the road ahead, then caught her lower lip between her teeth and looked into the rearview mirror. There he was, right behind her, holding her speed and staring straight into her mirror. Their eyes met, and he smiled, the slowest, sexiest smile she had ever seen. She couldn't believe it. No, she was imagining this! This kind of thing never happened to her!

Suddenly the stranger in the sports car signaled, pulled out, and began to pass her. There, she was right, she told herself; she had imagined the smile, the look. Now he'd zoom past her and disappear into his own future. Silly girl, imagining all kinds of—

Ooops! Her heart did a little somersault into her throat. There was the sports car, nose to nose, window to window alongside her, matching her speed exactly. Ellen swallowed hard and slid her glance sideways. The stranger smiled, white teeth flashing in his startlingly handsome face. It happened so quickly, like the snap of a photograph, but Ellen saw his chiseled features and dark, laughing eyes, a shock of black wind-ruffled hair. Blushing hotly, she pinned her eyes to the road, then weakened and looked over at him again. This time he merely held her eyes, waiting for her response.

She offered a tentative smile and a little lift of her shoulders.

She could almost hear his laugh; there was no mistaking his pleasure as he threw back his head, gave her an easy wink, and pulled the sports car ahead and back into her lane.

Ellen felt as giddy as a schoolgirl. She never did things like this, careless flirting with a stranger on the highway, but, oh . . . it was fun! She stayed behind him for five miles, watching him at sixty, the excitement of speed replaced by the excitement of watching him watch her in his rearview mirror. Then suddenly she saw him glance down, and his brake lights flashed on and off and on again.

Now what? she wondered, temporarily puzzled. Moments later they coasted by a police car, its radar aimed in their direction.

Repentance washed over her. And gratitude. What if she had been going eighty, screaming into the wind? That officer would have done more than give her a ticket she couldn't afford. He would have taken her away in his black-and-white and had her committed!

A shaky little laugh bubbled up in Ellen's throat. She waved out the window, wanting this knight in shining steel to know how grateful she was.

He waved back, a wide sweep of one bare forearm, the sunlight gleaming on his bronze skin. That easy gesture seemed so irresistibly sensual that Ellen felt her stomach tighten. Would he disappear now that his good deed was accomplished? She'd felt so wonderful for these past few minutes of fantasy—so fresh and alive and carefree! "Fate, be on my side for a change!" she yelled into the whip of the wind.

Damn! If *she* were in the lead, she would turn on her signal, flag him over to the side of the road, and introduce herself. It was all very brash and out-of-character, but she'd take the chance. She'd dare it this one time; maybe she'd be lucky.

Like magic his signal flicked on. He slowed, pulling off onto the shoulder, and then rolling to a stop.

Ellen followed as if in a dream.

She saw him step from his car and walk toward her, grinning. He was tall, maybe six feet or a little over, solidly built, but with lean hips and an easy, powerful stride.

Without a thought she opened her door and slid out, one hand gripping the windowframe for support. Her legs felt like spaghetti. She pushed her sunglasses up onto her dark hair and smiled. Her heart was beating wildly. "Hi!" She prayed that she looked as calm as she sounded.

"Hello. That was a close call back there."

"Oh, I know! Thanks for warning me; I would have hated a ticket just now—"

"I hate them anytime. There are too many better ways to spend money," he said lightly, but his dark gaze was resting on her face like a physical touch.

Ellen immediately had visions of dining by candlelight on rooftop terraces and dancing till dawn, held in his strong arms. Struggling for calm, she offered a little laugh. "I know what you mean. But how did you know the police were up ahead?"

He smiled. "A little gadget my friends installed to keep me out of trouble. I'd suggest that you get one, but I doubt if it would help at eighty-five miles an hour." His dark eyes flashed with amusement.

"Oh, I don't usually drive like that!" Ellen

insisted. "Really. I'm usually very safe and cautious."

One dark brow swooped up as if to point out that she was standing on the side of the road talking to a man whose name she didn't even know, a total stranger!

Quickly she shook her head, sending her brown hair flying around her face. There was more gold in it than he had thought . . . or perhaps the sunlight was playing tricks on him.

But when he lowered his eyes to hers, she held his glance and repeated firmly, "Really, I don't often do crazy things like this. I'm a very sensible person."

Armand looked deep into her eyes and felt the earnestness of that honest blue gaze. It was the truth then: She did not often smile at strangers, on the highway or elsewhere. *He* smiled.

"Good," he said, holding out his hand. "May I ask your name?"

"Ellen. Ellen Farrell," she answered, putting her hand in his. "And you?"

"Armand Dante." His smile widened. "And I am very pleased to meet you."

"Likewise." She started to laugh, delighting in the absurdity of it all, their mock formality there on the edge of the interstate, with the traffic whizzing by.

Matching laughter lit the depths of his dark eyes. "And at eighty-five miles an hour, Ellen Farrell, were you hurrying to work? Or to meet someone?"

"No, neither," she said, feeling the heat rise to her throat and cheeks. "No, I was just . . . just celebrating, I think. It's a beautiful day." She looked away, and her words trailed off into a shy smile.

He studied her face, the flush on her cheeks, her wide, wide blue eyes, that heart-stopping smile. "Wait here," he said, and strode back to his car. In a second he returned, holding a slim leather note-book and a fountain pen. "May I see you again? Will you give me your number? Your address?"

She was too startled to think. Too pleased to consider. He put the notebook into her hand and she opened it, flipping past pages of hastily sketched musical notation to an empty page.

She scribbled her name and address and handed the book back to him.

Immediately he read it aloud, his rich voice lending a strangely exotic quality to the familiar facts. Then he smiled at her, and her knees went from spaghetti to Jell-O. "I'll be seeing you again."

It was a line out of a movie. A deep, delicious lead-in, a tantalizing preview of wonderful, rapturous days and nights to come. Ellen held back a rising laugh. She had truly lost it; after all these weeks of too much work and too much turmoil, she was going crazy, retreating totally into a fantasy world! She felt her head bobbing gently, but no words seemed to come forth.

Armand Dante watched her slowly and carefully, his eyes sparkling. He seemed about to say more, but just then his gaze lifted to a point behind Ellen's head and he grinned, pulling her away from her delightful fantasy and back onto the rough easement of the highway.

"Looks like we have company. They probably

want to make sure I'm not holding you at gunpoint."

Ellen spun on her heel, and found herself staring at a police car that was rolling slowly to a stop just a few feet away. The officer was already leaning out his window, his eyes scanning the scene. "Everything all right here?"

Ellen gulped. "Oh, yes, sir. Everything's fine, thank you. You see, I pulled off to stretch my legs, and this nice man stopped to see if I was okay, and we're just fine."

"Good. That's all I wanted to know."

"Well," she said, laughing nervously, "I guess I'd better be going—"

"Don't let me chase you two away," the officer said.

Ellen's face flamed. "Oh, you're not! I've really got to go, but thanks again."

Armand was enjoying her every word and gesture. "I'll be seeing you soon," he said, not half as quietly as Ellen would have liked. "Good-bye." And with a wink he strode to his car.

" 'Bye," Ellen whispered. She climbed into her car, and edged back onto the highway right behind his sports car.

When they reached the next interchange, Armand pulled to the left, touched his forehead in a farewell salute, and raced on down I-95. Ellen picked up the Beltway and headed back home.

It was only as she drove over the light-dappled waters of the Potomac that she realized what she had just done. She had given her name—first and last—to a complete stranger! *Her address*. She, who knew there were crazy people out there, she, who worked with their victims every day in the hospital. Murderers and rapists and grafitti-scrawlers, men who dialed your number and breathed heavily at three A.M.! Panic gripped her; her heart seemed stuck in her throat, and her hands were clammy.

She tried to think calmly. That man, that gorgeous man, could never be a criminal. No, not with those warm dark eyes, that smile, that laugh. No, she was being silly. Or had she *been* silly and *now* she was being sensible? For the first time in her life she was absolutely and totally confused. Well, the second time if she counted her brief, impossible stint in the convent with Laurie. Oh, well, the third if she counted Dan.

Her life was falling apart!

Her lips trembled. Her hands trembled. When she parked the car at the curb, her knees buckled so she could hardly walk. Clarence saw her coming, and hurried to her side.

"Hey, Ms. Farrell, you're lookin' rotten. Are you okay?"

"No, Clarence!" Ellen gasped, leaning on his arm. "I've gotten myself into a little bit of difficulty. I—I gave this strange man my name and address—" She covered her face with her free hand, mortified to be telling all this to Clarence and too scared not to tell someone right away. "Would you please check in on me a couple of times today? And keep your eye out for a tall, dark-haired, very good-looking man?"

"Hey, just spread *that* word and everybody in this building will be on the lookout!"

"Clarence!"

"Sorry . . . just jokin'. You're really upset about

this fella, aren't you? Well, don't you worry. Clarence'll be your own personal watchdog."

"Right now I think I need a Saint Bernard . . . with a good full keg of brandy!"

Two

It took earthquakes to surprise Ellen Farrell, but Clarence's message definitely sent a jolt through her system.

"You've got whom? . . . Oh, no, Clarence! . . . Yes, yes . . . I know what I said, but . . ." Ellen's voice squeaked to a halt. In her wildest imagination she hadn't thought he'd show up. Not *really*. Dark, mysterious-looking strangers that one met on highways—especially incredibly handsome ones—reappeared only in dreams, *never* on doorsteps!

Stuffing her bare feet into a pair of slippers that stuck out from beneath the couch, Ellen made a beeline for the door. Visions of Clarence's well-muscled arm wrapped around the stranger's neck sent her racing down the narrow stairs.

"Oh, my Lord!" Ellen skidded to a stop in the small lobby, her heart clammering loudly against her ribs.

His feet glued to the tile floor, Clarence stood immobile while a figure in a dark wool overcoat resisted the viselike grip in which he found himself. A rather bedraggled bouquet of yellow roses was in his hand.

"It's you . . . it *is* you, isn't it?" Ellen peered down at the thick head of hair. Of course it was! No one else could have that head of hair, that wonderful, run-your-fingers-through-it dark wavy mane of hair that looked almost blue-black in the light of the entrance.

Straining, the man tried to raise his head to see her, but Clarence's judo hold made it physically impossible for him to see anything but the floor and a narrow stretch of wall in front of him.

When he spoke, he sounded short of breath. "Your voice . . . is right . . . but I'm . . . not sure. Would you consider screaming for me? I never forget a scream—" The man twisted again, his voice strained but tinged with a hint of amusement.

A sigh of relief escaped Ellen's lips. Thank heaven he had a sense of humor! she thought. Perhaps he wouldn't have her jailed or tarred and feathered for this, even though she knew she probably deserved it.

"Clarence, stop! It's okay!"

"Isn't this the right fella? Sure looked like your description, Miss Farrell!"

"No! I mean . . . yes, he does match it, Clarence—" She managed a lopsided smile. "You're a terrific detective. But on closer look I can see that this man couldn't possibly be dangerous. Please let him go, Clarence." The doorman immediately released his hold.

Uncurling himself from the position he had held

for the last few minutes, Armand Dante stood upright and stared long and hard into Ellen's wide, unwavering blue eyes.

Armand Dante wasn't known for his patience or for his mild-mannered ways; yet at this incredibly incongruous moment, when what he ought to do was break into one of his famous tirades, all he could do was shake his head and smile in a way that softened the chiseled angles of his handsome face.

"Well, Miss Farrell"—his voice was deep and low with almost a touch of the theatrical in it—"frankly, we've got to stop meeting like this!"

Ellen burst into laughter. "I—I'm so sorry, I—" She clasped her hand over her mouth as the laughter bubbled out unchecked, her eyes brimming with moisture. "I'd try to explain, but—"

"But it wouldn't make no sense anyhow!" Clarence warned, his hands staunchly on his hips but amusement in his voice. "Miss Farrell here, she certainly keeps things hopping! Sorry about this whole thing, Mr.—"

"Dante. And no need to apologize. You have quite a grip there, by the way." He shook the older man's hand firmly, his eyes glinting with humor. "It's been an interesting beginning to the evening." His glance shifted to Ellen. "Perhaps a portent of things to come?"

His look was so deep and probing, Ellen felt exposed, strangely unnerved, and—what was worse—intensely excited in a way that sent a flush spreading up over the neckline of her blouse to her cheeks.

She pressed a hand to her face, but stubbornly held his eyes. "You . . . well, why are you here?"

Armand grinned at her candor and handed her
the roses he had been holding. He had asked himself the very same question as he abandoned piles
of scores on his desktop and found his way to the
address she had written in his leather notebook.
He felt like a kid again, chasing fire engines, but he
couldn't tell her that.

"To bring flowers to a beautiful lady who brightened a dull day for me. And to ask that same lovely
lady if she'd have dinner with me."

"Dinner . . . ?" Ellen repeated, trying to sound
rational despite the rapid flutter of her pulse.
"Dinner?"

"Yes." He took hold of her elbow lightly and
turned her so she faced the door and the night
darkness beyond. "My car is parked right out
there—in a no-parking zone. I'd like to whisk you
off in it before I get a ticket, then dine with you by
candlelight."

Clarence nodded his head enthusiastically.
"Sounds good to me, Miss Farrell. You need a night
out!"

Ellen threw him a threatening glare. All she
needed now was one of Clarence's instant analyses
of her love life—or, as seemed to be the case, *lack* of
it!

"Well, that would be nice," she answered hur-
riedly, refusing Clarence time to intrude or herself
time to think. "Sure. Dinner sounds fine!"

She took his arm, guiding him away from the
doorman's interested, solicitous gaze.

Armand paused, a half-smile curving his lips.

"What's wrong?" Ellen asked. "Change your
mind or something?"

"No," he replied, his dark eyes skimming down

her body. "But perhaps you would like to change your shoes? Although those *are* very becoming on you." His voice was sexy and teasing.

Ellen glanced down; the rabbit ears attached to the front of her furry pink slippers seemed to bob in agreement. "Oh!" She laughed huskily and teased right back. "Of course; I nearly forgot. I almost never take Mopsy and Flopsy out to dinner." She grinned up at him from beneath the dark fringe of her lashes.

Armand Dante watched her carefully until their gazes melted together. And at that moment the fog lifted and suddenly, inexplicably, it made absolutely perfect sense that he should be standing in the drafty hallway of Ellen Farrell's apartment house, inviting her to dinner.

"I'm sorry, but I really will have to be home by ten-thirty." Ellen reluctantly glanced at her watch as the maître d' seated them at a linen-clothed table.

"Ah, I have a Cinderella on my hands!" Armand teased.

"Something like that." Ellen laughed, feeling wonderfully carefree. The short ride to the restaurant in the tiny sports car was all it had taken to completely dispel the feeling that Armand Dante was a stranger. She knew nothing about him, and everything that mattered, all in a mysterious way that defied time and logic and scrutiny. "Hmmm, where's my fairy godmother been hiding all this time?" The glow in her cheeks deepened to match the soft rosy hue of her silk blouse.

"Mr. Dante"—their waiter bowed slightly as he interrupted—"we are so pleased to see you."

Armand spoke pleasantly and familiarly with the waiter as Ellen looked on, her curiosity piqued. This was a lovely, expensive restaurant; she had been to it only once before, when her best friends, Laurie O'Neill and Rick Westin, had announced their wedding plans, and that had been three years ago. Armand, obviously, was a frequent patron.

After ordering a bottle of champagne, he turned his complete attention back to Ellen.

Perhaps he was right, she thought, returning his smile, she was beginning to feel a little like Cinderella! "Armand?" Her blue eyes were clear and direct. "Armand, you know this is really quite crazy, quite out of character for me. I mean, I usually don't—"

"—pick men up on the highway, and then subject them to Clarence's death grip?" He reached across the tabletop and covered her hand with his as tiny laughlines crinkled around his eyes.

"What? *You* were the one; *you* picked *me* up! And Clarence tends to be a little overprotective, that's all." She tried to ignore the tantalizing heat of his hand on hers. It wasn't easy!

"You are absolutely right," Armand agreed gallantly. "It was all my doing. And believe it or not, it was a first for me. I've never before fallen in love on route 495."

Ellen gulped, then decided this must be your normal candlelit-dinner banter. She joined right in. "Never? Where do you usually fall in love? Wisconsin Avenue? I usually prefer N Street. Although sometimes in the summertime old Highway 50 is absolutely irresistible—"

Armand touched her cheek softly with the tips of two fingers, and Ellen's words died in her dry throat.

"You're a surprise to me, Ellen. I'm not even sure quite what it is that sets you apart, but you are very special."

Ellen blushed. Her eyes flitted over his strongly sculpted features, then took refuge in gazing at the muted pattern of his tie. She'd always been well aware of her strengths and weaknesses: talking directly to people was definitely one of her strong points. But at that precise moment, as the waiter put a plate of delicately flavored clams between them, she felt less socially adept than she had at her freshman prom at St. Joseph's Academy back in Pittsburgh, Pennsylvania.

Reluctantly she slipped her hand free and took a sip of the dry, chilled champagne. It slid soothingly down her throat. She tilted her head back and faced him with feigned assurance. "Armand, you know nothing about me. Nothing. I could be a woman of the streets—"

He lifted one thick brow in amusement.

"—or a corrupt politician. Or . . . or someone who staked you out for your money."

Armand's grin was widening. "My money?"

Ellen's hand swept through the air, then pointed to his finely tailored suit as she spoke. "Well, sure. This restaurant. Your suit. Your car. You obviously *have* money." She sat back and smiled. "You really ought to be more careful, you know. Fortunately you were lucky. I'm safe." She leaned forward in her chair and smiled into his eyes.

Armand took that moment to recapture her hand. He loved touching her, feeling the yielding coolness of her skin beneath his touch. "You're safe? Ellen Farrell is safe?"

The way he said her name sent wonderful messages to her brain. It lifted plain "Ellen Farrell" to a lofty, delicious realm of fantasy and drama. A name fit for a queen. She giggled softly. "No, actually *you're* safe. With me. Now, whether or not I'm safe with you is an entirely new issue. Perhaps that's what we ought to be talking about!"

Her soft chestnut hair spilled over one shoulder as she leaned forward. Armand watched it as the glow of candlelight lifted highlights from the silken depths. It was beautiful hair, he thought, the kind to slide your fingers through or scoop up in your hand and press to your cheek. He smiled softly.

"You're safe with me, Ellen; I promise you. Don't doubt that for a minute."

But his eyes flashed in a way that made Ellen question his definition of safety and her own sanity as well.

She was rescued from trying to probe more deeply into his words. The waiter appeared to unobtrusively fill their table with platters of beef Wellington and crisp, colorful vegetables in delicate sauces.

They settled in, enjoying the dinner and each other; conversation flowed as easily as honey from a spoon. He loved waterfalls and skiing, oyster stew and Woody Allen movies. Ellen agreed, and discovered happily that Armand shared her craving for chocolate chocolate chip ice cream. They sparred on foreign policy, argued with heated enjoyment over current events. Ellen brushed her hair behind one ear and settled back into the soft chair, her face aglow. She felt childishly happy, giddy almost.

Only dim shadows of the past months of confusion clouded her mind.

After refilling her champagne glass, Armand raised his own to touch it. "To my charming Cinderella of the highway. May your glass slipper never break."

Ellen tipped her glass to his. A vision of the sturdy nurses' shoes waiting for her at home suddenly slipped into her mind, and she repressed the urge to laugh. "I'm sure it won't," she murmured softly, then sipped the champagne, finding an intense enjoyment in being toasted by Armand Dante. She faced him curiously.

"Your name . . . it's very familiar to me. Were you named after a literary character? Or someone I should know?" Ellen slipped a small forkful of tender meat into her mouth.

Armand laughed deeply. "Perhaps you're thinking of the poet. *Paradise Lost*?"

Ellen shook her head. "No, that's not it. Someone more contemporary—" She searched her mind but came up empty. Shrugging her shoulders, she smiled lightly. "Who knows, maybe we've met in another life."

"Never. How could I possibly have forgotten you?"

His flirting was soft and sensuous, not irritating, and Ellen found herself charmed.

"Sir—" The waiter was back, holding a piece of printed white paper. "If I might disturb you for a moment. A woman has asked me to request your autograph on this program. I wouldn't usually honor such a request, but—"

"But the woman happens to be married to your boss, right?" Armand looked up at the flustered waiter and winked, putting him at ease. At the same time he scribbled automatically on the program. "No problem, John."

Ellen watched the scene wide-eyed, then shifted in her seat to try to read the paper resting on the table.

Obligingly Armand turned it toward her.

"Armand Dante" was scribbled at the bottom.

"Your name . . ." she said almost to herself, her brows drawing together.

"Yes. My name. I don't believe in forgery."

Ellen's eyes scanned the sheet until they rested on the printed name that matched the signature: "Armand Dante, conductor. Virginia Symphony Orchestra."

She stared at him intently. A conductor! He didn't look like a conductor. Weren't they usually older . . . white-haired? The only images she could call to mind quickly were Leonard Bernstein, and Arthur Fiedler of the Boston Pops. Armand certainly didn't match either of those pictures.

He was intriguing-looking, definitely, with that faint shadow of a beard, his square-cut chin and his eyes so dark and deep, they seemed nearly black. An Italian soccer player, perhaps, or an unconventional movie star. But a conductor? She leaned her head to one side.

"You—you're Dante? Our conductor . . . here?" She felt absolutely foolish, but decided at that instant she could live more comfortably with irritation. "Why did you hide that from me?" she demanded.

"Hide it?" Armand laughed heartily. "Ellen, with a name like mine, one doesn't hide anything. How many *Armands* do you know? I told you my name—"

"But you didn't explain. I mean, you didn't remind me! Of course I knew of you. I just forgot, that's all. You should have said!" But silently she scolded herself. Everyone knew who Armand Dante was!

Armand's laughter wrapped around her like a warm cloak. "Ellen Farrell, you've never seen me perform, have you? You've never been to one of my concerts?"

Ellen caught her bottom lip between her teeth. Then, taking a deep breath, she met his laughing eyes. "Well, actually, no. I admit I never have. I don't know a lot about classical music." She shook her head until her hair spun around her face, then she tilted her chin up proudly. "But that doesn't mean I don't like music, of course. I have a dear friend, Rick Westin, who plays the banjo—"

"Rick Westin? Yes, I've heard him. He's a fine performer."

"Yes, he's wonderful. I understand *his* music. It tells a story, speaks to me. Classical music is something I've never really been exposed to, and I'm afraid it's beyond my grasp."

She offered a little smile of apology, feeling as though she'd just told him she didn't like his voice or that his hair was the wrong color.

Armand Dante was not disturbed, not in the slightest. Smiling gently, he reached over and touched her cheek. "That's nonsense. It certainly isn't beyond your grasp. But that's beside the point. You don't need to apologize for not listening to classical music. Certainly not to me."

"No, I'm not apologizing really. I just want you to understand. I mean—"

What did she mean? she wondered. She had loved every minute of this evening with Armand Dante. He had made her feel beautiful and special and alive. And should he, in a slight moment of insanity, decide to ask her out again, it was only fair that he be informed that her knowledge of classical music would fit on the tip of a pin! Which made the two of them as well-suited for each other as a square peg in a round hole.

Ellen prided herself on being realistic and honest—even when she didn't want to be! She pushed on.

"Well, what I mean is that this is all rather funny, isn't it? I mean, here you are, a well-known conductor—a celebrity actually—having dinner with me, a nurse who knows nothing about classical music and spends most of her time in the relative obscurity of the city hospital emergency room." She paused just long enough to look up and flash him a lovely smile. "We can both chalk it up to a strange, funny accident."

Armand Dante was leaning on the table, watching her with that particular intensity of his, his handsome face still and alert. "So, you are a nurse. That explains a lot."

"Well, it explains why I need to be home at ten-thirty; I have the graveyard shift tonight. You see," she teased softly, "I'm really not Cinderella after all."

Ellen felt a certain sadness, that pang that comes when waking from a wonderful dream and finding out none of it was real. In a few hours she'd be back at work at the hospital, and Armand Dante would vanish back into the dream of his world. But it had been a wonderful night. So, perhaps the sadness was worth it.

Unaware of her thoughts, Armand was pursuing his own. "I should have known you were a nurse, Ellen Farrell."

"Why? Do I have that Florence Nightingale look? Or is it my bedside manner?" She cupped her chin in her hand, her eyes wide and teasing.

Armand Dante laughed gently, but refused to be drawn out of his sudden seriousness. "Neither. There's a compassion in your eyes—a light. That's why I should have known."

"A light," Ellen repeated, her voice soft with pleasure. "Armand, I think that's from the wine, but thank you just the same for the lovely compliment. I have to admit, though, I'm a nurse practically by default. No heroics involved at all."

"Default?"

"Yes." She laughed huskily. "The choices presented to us back in high school were limited: nursing, teaching, or becoming a Sister of Divine Providence. I never wanted to be a teacher, and after six weeks in the convent it was mutually agreed that Ellen Farrell could best serve the church in another capacity—comedian, mother of twelve, longshoreman . . . whatever! So nursing seemed the most practical choice. And here I am."

Armand was laughing now, the sound rumbling from his broad chest. Ellen wondered fleetingly what it would be like to press her palms to the wall of his chest and feel those deep vibrations in her fingertips. Instead, she forced her eyes back to his face and grinned. "See, nothing so interesting here."

"You must be kidding! Tell me, were you really in a convent, Ellen?" He could not imagine this vivacious spirit being shrouded in a habit behind high walls.

"Yes." She tilted her head and smiled into his eyes. "And I loved it! For about five weeks. My closest friend, Laurie, went with me, and I spent the time bolstering her and the others up, clowning them out of their homesickness, and helping to keep their eyes on the glorious goal ahead. But suddenly it was time for *me* to concentrate on that goal and it scared me to death. I flew off with the blessings of my superiors hurrying my heels!" Her voice softened. "They knew, bless them, that there's a place for everyone . . . and the convent simply wasn't my place."

"Then your place is here, in Washington? Nursing?" Armand wanted her to go on talking so that he could go on sitting there, looking into her eyes; their sparkle seemed to light his soul.

Ellen answered honestly. "No. Not really. Oh, I'm content here for now, but there's a part of me that's not ready to say, This is it, this is where you belong, Ellen." Her eyes sought his. "I love the people I meet at the hospital, and I love doing something to better their lives. But life is such a wonderful sea of change that, well, who knows?" She flashed him a smile. "Who knows what tomorrow will bring?"

Reaching out, she touched his hand, then slipped her fingers between his. "But I do know what today brought: this lovely time with you. Thank you, Armand Dante. I shall think of you each time I go bananas along the highway, each time I read about one of your wonderful concerts,

each time—and it's often I assure you—I eat chocolate chocolate chip ice cream."

For a moment her smile seemed to waver in the
flickering light of the candles as she slipped her
hand back across the table. "It has been a lovely
evening, but now it's time to go."

"No, Mr. Rosen, I didn't get a new hairstyle,"
Ellen said laughingly as she adjusted the tube on
the elderly man's IV.

From beneath the crisp white hospital sheets the
semi-retired playwright scrutinized her with the
acuity born of his art. "Well, something's different;
that's as clear as this damn needle in my arm!"

"Now, Mr. Rosen, let's stay calm." Ellen wrapped
her fingers expertly around his thin wrist as she
took his pulse. A frequent hospital patient in the
past year, Elliott Rosen had wiggled his crochety
way right into Ellen's heart.

"Calm? What do you know from calm!" His tired
eyes sparkled as they teased her fondly. "You're as
high as a kite tonight. What're you on, Ellie, glue?"

His gruff laugh always surprised Ellen. It was
strong and vibrant, defying the cruel tricks nature
had played on his body.

"Nope." She grinned. "Beef Wellington and
strawberries Romanoff!"

The old man's thin brows shot up. "With a
man?"

"With"—Ellen patted his arm proudly—"Armand
Dante!"

Elliott Rosen lifted himself up on a bony elbow as
one brow arched wickedly. "Ellie, you're putting
me on."

Ellen's eyes sparkled. "No, Mr. Rosen, I'm not. Do you know who he is?"

"*Who he is?* Nurse Farrell, you ought to be ashamed of yourself to ask an idiotic question like that. Of course I know who he is!" His voice grew stronger. "The finest conductor alive, in my modest, but expert opinion." He lifted himself farther and shook a long, gnarled finger at Ellen. "He's a true artist, Armand Dante, and don't you forget it, young lady!"

Ellen's husky laughter warmed the sterile hospital room. Holding both hands out in front of her, she shook her head. "I'm not arguing, Mr. Rosen, honest. I only wish I knew as much about him as you seem to. I didn't even recognize his name!"

Elliott Rosen chuckled as he sank back into the bed. "That's what every star needs, a little of Ellie Farrell to put him in his place." He pulled the white sheet up under his chin. "Tell you what I'll do, sweetie; tomorrow I'll have some of his tapes sent up to me here and you and I will have a little lesson in appreciating some of the finer things in life."

That's just what tonight was! Ellen thought to herself. Aloud she answered, "Thank you, Mr. Rosen. I'd enjoy that."

"Good. And then when you see the gentleman again—"

"Oh"—Ellen's voice was small and wistful—"I don't think that will happen. Tonight was a fluke, just a wonderful fluke. He didn't mention seeing me again."

No. He had kissed her once, a sweet, light brush of his lips against hers at the door, and then with a small, oddly formal bow he was gone. And she had leaned against the doorframe, weak-kneed, filled with a strange trembling passion. The timbre of his voice, the depths of his dark eyes, the cool, starched linen of his shirt—she found them all compellingly attractive. But she'd probably never see him again.

"Of course you'll see him again!" Elliott Rosen insisted with great certainty. "Why, the man is single; he *needs* a good woman, and you, Ellie, are perfect! You hush now and don't argue with a sick man. Leave me, Ellie dear—I've things to think about." His head sank back into the pillow, and his lids slowly dropped.

Ellen watched him fondly for a second. Then, flicking off the light switch, she turned and walked softly toward the door. A faint sound drifted along behind her in the darkness. Pausing, Ellen listened carefully and quietly as Elliott Rosen drifted off to a peaceful sleep, humming the first movement of a familiar classical tune.

Three

The ticket came two days later, hand-delivered to the hospital by a somber-faced man in a chauffeur's uniform. It arrived just as Ellen was completing her shift and only minutes after she had convinced herself she'd never again hear from Armand Dante. He'd been a dream for a day, a phantom in the night. And now there were other things that needed her attention—like syringes and IVs.

"Farrell!" her friend Adeline had screeched, poking her mane of red hair into the nurses' locker room. "Someone is out there looking for you, Ellen. A guy in uniform! You've either got some real high-class friends you've been keeping a secret, or the government's after you!"

Ellen hurried out after the other nurse, then came to an abrupt halt in front of the emergency room desk.

"Ms. Farrell?"

"Who are you?"

"Are you Ms. Ellen Farrell?"

"Yes, I am."

"Then this is for you." He handed her a small pearl-gray envelope.

Ellen stood dumbfounded, feeling as if she had stumbled onto a movie set.

Adeline put her hands on her hips and cocked her head to one side. "Well, Ellen?" she prompted. "Aren't you dying to find out who it's from?"

Ellen stared at the other woman as if becoming aware of her presence for the first time. "Of course; yes!" she answered. She tore the envelope open and pulled out a matching sheet of heavy writing paper. A printed ticket slipped out with it and drifted down to the desktop.

"Well . . . ?" The other nurse tapped one toe on the linoleum impatiently. Mysterious notes were not a daily occurrence in the E.R., and one hand-delivered by a chauffeur was enough to initiate mild cardiac arrest.

Ellen swallowed the huge lump in her throat and silently read the wonderful scrawled message:

My dear Ellen,

It would bring me great delight and pleasure to have you attend Saturday night's concert as my special guest. Your ticket is enclosed. I hope, my Cinderella, that you will not have to run off at 10:30.

Yours,
Armand

She didn't realize she was holding her breath until it escaped in a sudden gasp.

"Oh, my Lord." The words were spoken with such astonishment that Adeline looked anxiously at her friend.

"You okay, Ellen?"

Ellen looked up. She felt a thin beading of sweat on her face and forehead, and her heart was beating crazily. "Oh, Adeline, I don't know. I really don't know. . . ."

Saturday arrived just about the time Ellen ran out of excuses.

"No, I simply can't go. I have to work Adeline's shift—"

"My dishwasher is acting up and I don't want to leave it alone, just in case—"

"There's an old Boris Karloff movie on TV I've waited years to see—"

"Mass. That's it! I'm going to Saturday night mass. You can't argue with God, after all."

They sounded ridiculous, even to her, and she was desperate. "Oh, Ellen Farrell, you're acting like a jerk, you know," she scolded herself out loud. She wrinkled her smooth forehead at the reflection in the mirror, and tried her most persuasive voice. "Mr. Rosen says this is going to be one of the best concerts of the season." She smoothed the silky peacock-blue dress over her slim hips. "It will be wonderful, he said. Rimsky-Korsakov, Dvorak—" She felt the unfamiliar names roll off her tongue as Mr. Rosen had taught her. "An *honor*, he said."

Then why was her stomach tied so tightly in knots that it hurt? she wondered.

Even Laurie and Rick thought she was overreacting. Goodness, hadn't Laurie gone to a concert of Rick's all alone? But Rick's music was . . . well, it was wonderful, folksy, *understandable*. She was as comfortable at Rick's concerts as she was with Rick. But Armand Dante? *He* was a whole different story.

But it was too late now. Backing out a half hour before the curtain was scheduled to rise was unacceptable.

She glanced back into the mirror one last time, practiced what she hoped was a concert-type smile, and headed out into the night.

By the time she got out of the taxi at the music hall, Ellen had calmed down considerably. It was simply a concert, a new experience. She had liked Arthur Fiedler, after all. And at least she didn't have to worry about what to say to Armand Dante. The maestro would have more important things than Ellen Farrell on his mind.

She smiled back at a well-dressed usher and followed him down the carpeted aisle of the hushed concert hall. Three-quarters of the way down the center aisle he paused and motioned toward an empty seat.

"There you are, madam, Mr. Dante's special row." He smiled knowingly, and Ellen looked over at the seat, then back to the usher.

"Mr. Dante's row?"

"Yes, ma'am. Some of the finest seats in the house—the acoustics, you know." And he moved smoothly off to the end of the aisle.

As she settled herself into the plush velvet seat, Ellen promptly forgot about acoustics and concentrated instead on the well-dressed people filling the row on either side of her. There was an elderly couple, the woman looking fine and proper in her furs and jewels. And a younger couple who were reading the program with educated smiles on their faces. Were they also friends of Armand's? And what about the elegant gray-haired woman on the aisle seat chatting with a striking blonde in a black evening dress and a handsome gentleman in a dark suit.

Because no one seemed to be wondering about her, Ellen finally shifted her attention forward to the formally dressed orchestra members sitting on the stage tuning their instruments. Her eyes moved with interest over the strings and bass instruments, then to the empty podium in the center of the stage. She smiled as her imagination conjured up an image of Armand, dark and poised and handsome, standing there with hands raised, ready to begin the concert.

Oh! Her hand moved to her cheek and Ellen's eyes widened. No, she couldn't sit here, this wouldn't work at all. Glancing around the hall, she spotted a cluster of seats closer to the stage and far off to the left. A few scattered people dotted the area, but most of the seats were empty. Yes! That would be much better. Standing quietly, she leaned forward and shuffled her way back to the aisle just as the houselights began to blink.

"Ma'am?" the usher was at her side. "The performance is about to begin. May I be of help?"

Ellen smiled brightly and shook her head. "I don't think so. Are those seats over there taken?"

With an indulgent smile the man explained that they were almost always left empty. "They are not choice seats such as yours, madam. Certainly nothing Mr. Dante would ever consider for his guests."

Ellen kept her smile in place and listened politely, her mind racing on ahead. No, perhaps Mr. Dante wouldn't have chosen them, but then, Mr. Dante lived and breathed his music. Mr. Dante didn't need visual aids to help guide him through the evening. But Ellen Farrell certainly did! "Watch his face," Elliott Rosen had instructed. "Watch and listen, Ellie, and your mind and heart will see. . . ."

Ellen flashed the usher a courteous smile and stood tall, her shoulders back. "I understand, but I can't see his face from here." She smiled matter-of-factly and hurried over to the other side of the auditorium.

Just as Ellen slipped down into an empty seat in the first row, the lights dimmed and the stage became an island of brightness. Conversation died away and a feeling of expectation grew and filled the hall.

Ellen wet her lower lip with the tip of her tongue. This was exciting somehow. Not like Rick's casual concerts where people sauntered in and out and, as often as not, Rick entered the crowded room already strumming on his banjo. Here there was a spine-tingling feeling of hushed anticipation.

Then, at exactly the right moment, Armand Dante strode from behind the maroon curtains at the wings and walked deliberately toward the low podium at the center of the stage. Strong applause began even before he appeared, and grew until he arrived at the middle of his world.

Ellen swallowed quickly, her heart pounding. He was beautiful, a dark, dramatic figure in white tie and tails. The stagelights caught the shining glint in his dark, mysterious eyes.

Ellen strained to see the sheets of music he'd be using, but the music stand was missing. Applauding with the others, she leaned toward the woman next to her.

"Doesn't he use music?"

Over the din her neighbor graciously replied, "He memorizes his scores, dear. Only two or three conductors can do that and get away with it, and he's one of them."

Ellen settled back, absorbing the information slowly. She wasn't sure exactly what it meant, but it definitely didn't calm the butterflies inside her or bring Armand Dante down to life size. She raised her eyes and focused on the stage.

Dante bowed, turned to the orchestra, and waited. A hush fell over the audience. She watched his arms rise gracefully to chest height, a movement as smooth and practiced as that of a fine dancer. His eyes moved from the concertmaster on his left to the harpist beyond. And then, with a baton movement so slight she almost missed it, he brought the opening bars of the music gloriously to life.

Releasing a slow breath, Ellen stole a quick glance at the program. *Scheherazade*, by Rimsky-Korsakov: the story of a prince and princess in love.

"Watch his face." Mr. Rosen's words drifted across her mind once again. Ellen watched as she listened, watched his face, his thick-browed, expressive eyes, his smooth, sure hands, his broad and graceful shoulders beneath his jet-black coat. As the delicate, sinuous melody drew her slowly into its distant magic, she found herself drifting off into a lovely blend of fantasy and beauty.

Images of the young princess, lonely, unfulfilled, and wistful, filled the stage. Ellen dared not blink, afraid the figures would vanish before the tale was told.

Armand's eyes were closed, his eyebrows slightly raised, his skin dark and smooth above the collar of his shirt. The slight, controlled movements of his baton conjured up other images, images that continued to grow on their own.

As the entire orchestra joined in and repeated the lush melody, Armand's face grew intense, scowling with concentration and emotion. Ellen sat forward, her eyes never leaving his face as he leaned and swayed, directing his players, cueing some to enter with his right hand, hushing another group with his left. His power and passion flowed from the stage and enveloped her in its embrace.

Armand Dante *became* the music, and Ellen couldn't take her eyes off him.

With the applause ringing in her ears she sank back into her seat. Her forehead was damp with a thin sheen of perspiration, and she felt suddenly exhausted.

Rick's music had been understandable, with words and music that spoke of earthy people and feelings she knew and understood. But this was different, a world apart, a world created by the mind and ear and heart. Ellen didn't begin to understand it all, but watching Armand this way had been more exciting than she could have imagined.

Armand was bowing now, deep and graceful, his

hair falling slightly forward as his firm body bent at the waist. She watched his eyes, his deep, black, wonderful eyes. They looked out over the applauding, well-dressed crowd, seeing everyone and no one, then traveled back through the rows until they paused just off center.

Ellen's breath caught in her throat. He was looking toward her reserved seat, her empty reserved seat.

The intensity in his eyes deepened, and for just a second Ellen thought she saw a flash of emotion. Then he lifted himself straight and tall once more.

Shivering, she rubbed her arms briskly.

"Are you cold?" her neighbor asked kindly. "You may borrow my sweater."

"No, I'm fine. It was just a sudden draft."

"Well, the second part of the program will warm you up, sweetie. I have a recording of Mr. Dante doing this one, and it's terrific."

A movement on the stage caught Ellen's attention then, and she and her neighbor looked up to see Armand Dante walking toward the wings. He was coming so close to them, Ellen felt she could reach up and touch his pants leg if she had the nerve. His eyes were lowered, his hands moving in slow motion at his side.

He had almost reached the wing curtain when something caused him to look up—up, then out, and directly into the waiting gaze of Ellen Farrell.

Only Ellen noticed the brief pause, the puzzled look in his eyes. But everyone in the lonely section tucked under the lip of the stage saw the darkly handsome smile that lit the face of the maestro then, and they all watched with delight as he nodded slightly, before disappearing from sight behind the velvety stage curtain.

It was later, during the intermission, that the usher found Ellen and handed her the note. She pressed one hand against her heart as she unfolded it and saw the handwriting that was becoming quickly as familiar to her as her own:

My dear Ellen,
    Please meet me backstage at the end of the performance.

                              Yours,
                              Armand
P.S. What are you doing sitting in that dreadful section?

Ellen bit back a smile.

The matronly-looking woman sitting next to her smiled knowingly. "I can tell from looking at you, sweetie, one of those orchestra musicians is your honey. Good choice in a mate, if I dare say so, but perhaps you could press him for better seats next time." Her voice drifted off in a motherly way.

Ellen pulled her eyes from the message to look at her companion. "Not mate. No, not in a million years. But a very nice friend. Armand Dante."

The woman's rough hand patted Ellen's knee, and she chuckled just as the lights dimmed for the final time. "Sure, dearie, and I'm Elizabeth Taylor. Now hush, child, while Mr. Dante and Dvorak fill our souls."

Fill our souls. The words lingered in Ellen's mind long after the music ceased and the noise of the applause reverberated throughout the crowded hall. Was that the reason for the tightness in her chest and the warm languid feeling that coursed slowly through her veins? Was that what Armand Dante was doing to her, filling her soul?

The thought sent shivers up and down her arms, and she tossed her coat over her shoulders as she rose from her seat. After taking a deep, steadying breath, Ellen bid her friendly companion good-bye and nudged her way toward the exit door near the edge of the stage. This must be the way backstage, she decided determinedly.

The last time Ellen had been backstage in a theater was when she was playing Peter Pan in the St. Joseph Academy's senior play. She remembered the production vividly and in minute detail because one of the cables had slackened just as she began her dramatic entry, propelling her like a sack from heaven into a stage-prop bush.

She'd pulled herself promptly from the tangled mess, informed the audience she was simply putting them at ease, and finished the performance, sprained ankle and all, to "critical acclaim" in the school newspaper.

A lifetime ago, she thought with a smile. And here she was, in her sophisticated, sexy dress, going off to have a brief tête-à-tête with none other than Armand Dante. "Ah," she murmured to no one in particular, "what tangled webs . . ."

"Miss Farrell?"

The same usher who had handed her the message stood in the hallway beyond the exit. He was a young man and stood so stiffly, Ellen had a sudden urge to salute.

Instead, she smiled brightly. "Yes?"

"This way, please. The maestro is waiting."

By this time Ellen felt light-headed and just this side of giddy. The maestro . . . is waiting. What lovely sounds the words made. Like *Dvorak* . . . and *Rimsky-Korsakov.* She smiled dreamily and followed the uniformed man through a door and down a hallway bustling with musicians. Light spilled out of an open doorway, and the man motioned her through it.

Ellen froze. She'd been moving through a dream, but this was all too real. What in heaven's name was she doing walking into Armand Dante's dressing room?

"Ma'am, are you all right?" The usher looked at her pale face with concern.

Ellen looked up slowly, then toward the open door. "No, I feel awful," she murmured. "Scared to death." With every ounce of energy left in her slender body she braced herself and forced a smile into place. "But when in Rome . . ." And with that she walked stiffly into the room.

"Ellen!" Armand spotted her immediately and broke away from the crowd of people pressing around him in the tiny dressing room. "At last!" He scooped her into the curve of his arm before she could say a word and pressed her close to him.

The warmth of his body was electrifying. If this were a dream, Ellen knew she'd awaken soon. The sounds and sights were so intense, no one could sleep through them.

"Hello, Armand." She swallowed around a giant lump. "The concert was lovely—"

Armand watched her face, and his own broke into an amused smile. "Ah, you liked it?"

"Yes." Ellen tipped her chin up, smiling more confidently now. "Especially the Dvorak."

"Wonderful! You're a hopeless romantic, just as I suspected." His eyes twinkled merrily, but he didn't press her. Instead, he swept her around until she faced the cluster of people waiting in the room.

"Friends, here she is: my lovely Cinderella of the highway!"

Six pairs of eyes moved slowly over her, from the top of her shining head of hair to her high-heeled shoes which were beginning to pinch in several places.

Ellen immediately focused on their guarded smiles as she took in the group: a pudgy, bald-headed man who accompanied his grin with puffs from a cigar, the elegant gray-haired lady she had seen in Armand's choice seats, and the young couple with the educated smiles. The orchestra's solo violinist and another musician completed the group.

"Well, well, well." The cigar-smoking man pumped Ellen's hand enthusiastically. "So this is Ellen. Happy to make your acquaintance. I'm Ted Sloane, Armand's manager, friend, and guardian angel."

Ellen liked him immediately. He was normal, she decided. The others were guardedly friendly and very sophisticated. A challenge.

Ellen tilted her head and answered their questions with a vibrancy that amazed even herself. She might not know classical music, but she knew people, and how to entertain them!

Armand's arm never rose from her shoulders, his eyes never left her face, and in moments she was chatting and laughing and toasting musical success with a delicate stemmed glass of champagne. From the society matron to the two musicians, they seemed to accept her there in their intimate circle. What if they discovered she had flunked high school chorus? she thought with a sudden giggle. Or that Rick had had to tell her Rachmaninoff wasn't a rock singer? Her lovely smile widened, and for the moment at least, held in the circle of Armand's arm, none of that mattered at all.

"Armand, it's been a lovely, wonderful, memorable evening." Ellen pressed comfortably against his side as they walked slowly toward his car.

"And you, Ellen Farrell, were the hit of the party."

Ellen laughed huskily. "Yes, and for one reason only, Armand Dante. Because you were there beside me, smiling at me and making them all wonder who in the world I was—and what in heaven's name I was up to!"

Armand tightened his hold on her as he looked up at the late night sky. "It was obvious who you were. The most charming, most beautiful woman there."

Ellen felt a soft heat rise to her face. Was she lovely? She certainly felt it tonight. Beautiful and exotic and wonderfully full of surprises.

Armand had swept her from the music hall to a post-concert party at a charming old house in Virginia. She'd been introduced and smiled at and sought out the whole night through, but deep down she knew very well why. It wasn't at all because she was Ellen Farrell. It was because she was on the arm of Armand Dante, who didn't for a moment let her out of his sight. But it didn't matter. Not tonight. For tonight the fantasy was going to be hers.

Ellen tilted her head back and smiled. "Thank you for a very special evening. It really has been, you know."

Armand paused beside his car and cupped her chin in the hollow of his palm. "Not 'has been,' Ellen. The music isn't over yet."

His eyes sparkled with the brilliance of a whole galaxy. Ellen felt herself drowning in their depths. "Isn't over? Armand," she said weakly, her heart pounding frantically, "do you realize it's almost dawn?" The whisper of her voice drifted off until she wasn't sure she had spoken.

"That's what I want to show you, Ellen. Dawn, the sunrise."

"Armand," Ellen gasped, laughing to hide the emotion that welled in her heart. "I've seen sunrises. Lots of them."

Armand opened the car door silently and motioned her in. His face was so close, she could feel his soft breath warming her cheek.

"But never with me, my Ellen. You've never seen a sunrise with me. It will be magnificent. Trust me. . . ."

The ground was cool, even through the soft wool blanket Armand had spread beneath them on the gentle rise of land. And the earth was quiet all around them, with the sleeping city off in the distance and the blinking stars beginning to fade in the sky above them.

Armand had removed his tuxedo jacket and

wrapped it loosely around Ellen's shoulders, then drawn her gently into the curve of his arm as the two sat watching the eastern sky slowly lighten.

"Armand, why did I let you talk me into this, I wonder? Am I under some kind of spell?" She tilted her head back and looked into his eyes to catch the smile she knew would begin there.

"No, my Ellen. You're a very romantic, adventurous soul, and you wanted to be here with me, watching a new day come into our lives."

She felt the rough dark hairs on his arm brushing gently against her neck. "Maybe. Maybe I am adventurous, but only in an ordinary sort of way. And you, Armand, are certainly not ordinary." She wrapped her arms around her knees and looked off into the soft hazy horizon. "But you are a new experience—"

"Ah, so that's what I am to the lovely Nurse Farrell, an *experience.*" His low, rumbling laugh drifted into the eerie quiet of the dawn.

Ellen smiled thoughtfully. "You most certainly are that. And what else are you? *Who* are you, Maestro Dante?"

"I am what you see, Ellen. Nothing else."

"Just an ordinary kid from Anywhere, U.S.A., who happens to be a famous conductor, leading a first class orchestra," Ellen teased gently.

"No, not anywhere. Dayton, Ohio."

Ellen cast him a suspicious glance. "Dayton, Ohio?"

"Yes, but just briefly." Armand bent one leg up and wrapped his free arm around it. "You see, my parents were quick to discover my musical 'gifts,' as they referred to them, and soon I was off to a private boarding school at the age of eleven, then Juilliard, and then—"

"—the rest is history?" Ellen laughed softly.

"Something like that." Armand reached over and lightly touched her cheek.

"It must have been difficult for your parents to send you away when you were so young," Ellen said. Thoughts of her own noisy, loving family filled her, and she knew without a doubt that no matter how talented any of the six Farrell children had been, her mother would never have allowed any of them to wander from the roost.

Armand was quiet for a moment. When he spoke again, his voice was husky and thoughtful. "I don't know if it was difficult for them, Ellen; we never discussed it. But it was very difficult for me. I missed my sister terribly. And rough-housing with the neighborhood kids. Fishing and playing ball, getting into mischief . . . that kind of thing." One finger slipped up to her cheek and rubbed it softly while he continued to speak. "I love music; it's my life. But there are times when—"

Ellen stole a look at his face as she waited for him to go on. His dark brows loomed thick above thoughtful eyes, his strong nose straight and sculpted above the darker shadow of his chin. When he spoke again, he seemed a million miles away.

"They gave me many things, my parents. And I'm grateful. But when I think about the family I would like to have some day, I know it will be different."

"Different? How, Armand?" Ellen asked softly. To her, families meant sprawling frame houses with kids on porches, mothers cradling babies and dads out throwing baseballs or loading the car with assorted and sundry children for a surprise trip to the ice cream store. They were ordinary-looking men, who went to work in the daytime. They weren't Armand Dante!

Armand laughed slowly with a huskiness that sent shivers running down Ellen's spine. "I can tell from watching you that you don't see me as a family man, Ellen."

"No. I guess I don't, Armand. Your life is so . . ."

"So what?" He cupped her chin in the palm of one hand and looked steadily into her eyes. "What *is* my life like?"

Ellen pondered the question carefully, her eyes locked into his. She neither blinked nor glanced away, but looked steadily into his gaze. "I don't know, Armand. I only know what it seems to be, and that is exciting, magical almost, something that would take my breath away and leave me dizzy and dreaming!"

His hand slid from her chin and flattened gently against her cheek. "No, my Ellen," he breathed into the diminishing space between them. "That's not my life. But maybe that is love. And maybe you'll share it with me."

His lips were soft when they pressed upon hers, soft as the dewy mist that drew the stars into its folds. And when Ellen felt the gentle sweep of his tongue as it traced the curve of her lips, she wound her arm around his neck and pressed closer.

The black jacket slipped from her shoulders and fell unnoticed to the ground.

Armand Dante's kiss was all she had dreamed it would be: daring, deeply moving, and mysterious. Ellen felt herself spinning and held on to him, unable and unwilling to slip from the web he was weaving about her.

"Trust me," he had said. The words floated somewhere in the very back of her mind, echoing, fading away, then slowly coming back again. His lips captured hers, more eager now, and an incredible heat rose up within her. His kisses became more demanding, deeper, as his hand slipped from her cheek to the side of her silky dress, resting on the gentle outer swell of her breast and then tracing the fan of her ribs.

A sigh fluttered in her throat. It was only a kiss, but she ached with a wild, sudden desire. It was as if she had never been kissed before, never known the rough velvet of a man's mouth, the heart-stopping daring of parting her lips to let his tongue dart in and capture hers. He tasted so sweet, so delicious.

Then why couldn't she breathe? Why was her heart pounding so?

She felt his hands behind her, those strong, sensual hands circling at the small of her back and then climbing the fragile column of her spine. He pushed his fingers into the dark cloud of her hair and tilted her head back, drawing her face up, up into his kiss. He stirred her so that she knew suddenly she would weep, and to hide it she broke from his arms and buried her face in her hands. She couldn't take it . . . not this glory, not the inevitable disappointment.

"Ellen," he whispered tenderly, leaning over her. "Ellen, look at me. Talk to me."

She heard the ragged edge of his breathing and felt a swift stab of contrition. "I—I'm sorry, Armand. I don't know what came over me. Sometimes I'm known for my silliness." Her eyes were huge and shining, filled with confusion.

"It's all right, my love. Don't be afraid. I won't push you." He drew her gently within the circle of his arm, turning her slightly to face the east. "Look. It's dawn."

Gone was the graying mist, and in its place was a paradise of color, a sky streaked with dusty pink and blue and purple and rosy gold and green and yellow. The silent sunrise was so moving, Ellen released her breath in a soft, slow gasp. "Armand . . . oh, Armand, I'm so glad to be here with you for this moment."

He pulled himself up, then drew her up beside him, a wonderful smile lighting his face.

"Didn't I tell you to trust me? This is the only way to end a glorious evening . . . and begin something more."

Four

"Farrell?" the nurse at the admitting desk repeated, her eyes lingering on the long narrow pristine white box with the huge pink bow.

"Yup," the delivery boy answered, reading from the invoice in his hand. "Miss Ellen Farrell, R.N., City Memorial Hospital." He pointed to the sign above the double doors to his right.

"This is the place." The nurse sighed, wishing the flowers were for her. "Go on in. Ask at the emergency room desk—"

The boy touched two fingers to his cap, cradled the box in his arms, and stepped through the double doors.

It was just after midnight, and things were quiet in the E.R. as white-coated doctors and uniformed nurses moved efficiently from one curtained room to the next. The delivery boy sidestepped a gurney carrying a very pregnant lady and headed for the desk as directed.

"Ellen Farrell, please? Flowers."

"Whooee! Hey, Ellen—a surprise!"

"In a second," Ellen called over her shoulder, and finished filling out an admittance form for a tiny woman whose husband had been brought in with chest pains. "Don't worry now, Mrs. Levy, everything will be fine. Why don't you sit down and I'll call you when we're ready to take your husband upstairs." She patted the frail old hand.

"Thank you, dear. I was so worried—"

"Of course you were. But the doctors are with your husband and everything will be fine now. And *you* need to rest a bit."

She offered a comforting smile, pushed some loose strands of hair back under her starched cap, and hurried to the front of the desk. "Adeline, did you call me?"

Before the other nurse could answer, the delivery boy set the elegant box onto the counter in front of her. "Ellen Farrell?"

Ellen just stared at it. "For me?"

"Invoice says Ellen Farrell, R. N."

"That *is* me." She nodded, her breath issuing from her throat in a little laugh of surprised delight. "I—I wasn't expecting flowers. Thank you. Do I—do I have to sign anything or—"

"Nope, that's it. Just enjoy 'em." He tapped his cap and turned to go.

"Oh, wait!" Ellen dug into her empty pockets and whispered nervously to Adeline, "Got a dollar? Anything?"

"Not a cent."

"Oh, darn," Ellen groaned. "Listen, I'm terribly

sorry, but my purse is in my locker and I don't have anything for a tip."

"Don't you worry about that, ma'am. It's already been taken care of. Well taken care of!" He grinned and dropped his voice to a conspiratorial hush. "Listen, the guy who ordered these paid a small fortune to have them delivered in the middle of the night. A few more deliveries like this and I can put a deposit on that motorcycle I've been wanting!" With a wink he was gone.

Ellen stood still for a moment, her heart pounding. Then the other nurse nudged her in the ribs. "Ellen, aren't you gonna open them? We're dying!"

"Yeah!" came a chorus of agreement from the group now gathered around the desk.

Ellen touched the pink bow. She let her fingers rest there briefly, memorizing the smoothness of the satin. She was filled with a sweet, unfamiliar feeling of anticipation. Then she pulled the ribbon off and opened the box.

Eighteen long-stemmed roses lay cradled in tissue. The roses were all the softest, most perfect pink, a dusty, dreamy pink seen only in the sky at sunrise, just before the sun peers over the horizon. They were beautiful, so beautiful, they brought tears to her eyes.

"Oh, how romantic!" Adeline sighed. "Tickets to concerts, roses. What's next?"

One of the interns whistled. "And *my* girlfriend thinks I'm a sport when I bring daisies from the supermarket. Whoever this guy is, keep him under lock and key!"

Ellen laughed softly. With trembling fingers she

lifted the tiny envelope and slipped out the card. It read:

To Ellen, who owned the rose-kissed world with me at sunrise—

Armand

Happiness brought a blush to her cheeks. She'd never felt like this before. No one had ever done anything so romantic for her. She'd dreamed of it, wished it, longed for it, but romance had always kept clear of the narrow, predictable path of her life. And here she was, stepping right into a fairy tale that was spinning romance around and around her until she was so dizzy she could barely think straight. She caught her breath and nipped her bottom lip in excitement. Here was the most romantic thing she'd ever imagined, and it was happening to her!

Quickly she knocked on a wooden chairback for luck, crossed her fingers, and whispered a silent prayer that it wouldn't end before she had tasted it more fully. Oh, please, don't let it end like last time. And then she thought of Armand's dark shining eyes, and that smile that made her heart stop, and the taste of his lips . . . and she banished her fears and tossed her head. "Well, anybody got a Waterford vase for these beauties?"

Someone handed her an empty plastic bottle used for IV solution, and she laughed and placed the roses in it. Their scent filled the E.R. with an exquisite sweetness. Cupping her hand, she held one bloom to her cheek, her eyes closed. Then she straightened her cap and went back to work.

Mrs. Levy and her husband were taken upstairs; a little girl was admitted with a broken leg caused by falling out of the top bunk at a sleepover, and Ellen had to calm both mother and child; then she helped stitch up the loser in a barroom brawl. It was a fairly typical night.

And through it all she stole glances at the roses. *Her* roses. And thought of Armand.

Perhaps it was *because* she was thinking about him that she didn't faint with surprise when he walked in the emergency room door. For a moment she believed she had conjured him up like a genie! But even her wildest fantasies couldn't have made him so incredibly perfect, lean and elegant in white tie and tails, his dark eyes flashing.

He halted in the doorway, coolly surveyed the scene, and found what he was looking for: her.

Armand crossed the room, took her in his arms, and kissed her passionately. His mouth was warm and demanding, and Ellen felt her toes curl inside her white nurses' shoes.

"Wait . . . stop!" she gasped. "What are you doing?"

"Oh, you forget so easily." He grinned, brushing his lips across the tip of her nose.

"No!" she said laughingly, her heart somersaulting to her throat. "I mean what are you doing *here*?"

"*You* are here."

"But I'm working!" she whispered, glancing over his shoulder at her open-mouthed colleagues. "You can't just come in here and kiss me—"

"All right. I'll have the limo run over me. Wait here."

She caught him from behind, wrapping her arms around his waist. "No, that is *not* necessary!"

He turned, all of his lean, hard body circling within her arms, and grinned at her. "Good. I'd hate to ruin this coat."

"You do look very handsome," she breathed.

"And you look beautiful," he answered softly.

"Me? In this uniform? Oh, Armand, don't be silly!"

He threw back his head and laughed. "I've been called many things in my life, but silly? Now I'll just have to prove to you how serious I am."

He lowered his face to hers, but Ellen ducked her head under his chin. "Armand, no, really, not here."

"Why not?" He laughed teasingly against her hair. "Embarrassed to be seen with me?"

The absurdity of that made her gasp. "Never! Oh, Armand, if anything, I'm flattered. And amazed. What does a man like you see in someone like me?"

His laughter died in his throat. Commandingly he tipped up her chin and made her look into his dark, intense eyes. "Don't say that. Don't *think* it. I'm just a man, a man who happens to be lucky enough to work at something that brings him great pleasure and satisfies a great passion. But I think that you are equally good at what *you* do, and perhaps your work is of even greater value. Don't think because I interrupted you here that I think little of what you do. It was only that I couldn't wait any longer to see you, touch you again."

Ellen stared up at him, amazement and happiness shining in her eyes, until Armand chuckled softly again and tapped her mouth closed with one blunt fingertip. "Don't look so surprised. You're a treasure, even if you don't know it. And I'll be happy to prove it to you."

She wanted to say, Yes, yes, make me believe you, prove it now! She wanted to cling to him, to rip off his perfect bow tie, slide her hand beneath his crisp white shirtfront and touch his warm flesh. She felt desire tear through her like a storm through a sheltered glade. But she was on duty, and duty called.

"Armand, I *have* to get back to work."

"And I have to get back to a cocktail party I fled rather abruptly. I left my hostess with my champagne glass in her hand, a rather startled look on her face, and thirty guests who are making handsome donations to the Symphony. But I'm glad I stole this minute with you." He brushed her cheek with the backs of his fingers. "I'll call you soon."

He strode through the double doors and was gone. Ellen leaned against the desktop for support, her mouth a perfect "O" of surprise.

One of the nurses took a quick look at her and laughed. "Wow! Who *was* that masked man, anyway?"

"I—I hardly know." Ellen said, stuttering.

"Well, when you find out, ask him if he has a brother!"

"Or a father!" laughed one of the older nurses.

"Wow!"

At 7:20, when the rest of the city was hurrying to get ready for work, Ellen was on her way home, bouncing lightly up the stairs to her apartment, her arms full of dusty-pink roses. The phone was ringing and she unlocked the door and made a dash across the room. "Hello?"

"Good morning, Cinderella."

Blood pressure rocketing! Pulse erratic! "Oh, Armand, it's—it's you! Oh, you are such a surprise!"

She heard that deep, husky chuckle of pleasure. "No more than you. I just wanted to say hello and wish you sweet dreams."

"Thank you." She grinned, knowing exactly what she'd be dreaming about. She blushed as if he could see her and quickly added, "What's *your* day like?"

"Terrible! Rehearsals all day. We're performing the Shostakovich Violin Concerto No. 1 on Saturday night, and I can't get them to feel the intensity. It's a wonderful piece, full of Slavic melancholy, and now it's lying like a wet blanket on the floor at my feet, and—" The passionate flood of words was suddenly dammed by a rueful laugh. "*And*, you probably didn't want to hear all that."

"Oh, but I *did* or I wouldn't have asked! Honest, I may not know a lot, but I'd like to learn."

"And I would like to be the one to teach you!" There was a pause heavy with meaning, and then his rich baritone came through the wire again. "I must go, and I don't know when I'll get to a telephone again. There's a business meeting tonight, and I'm leading the Youth Symphony in Arlington Wednesday night, a favor to an old friend. So—"

"So have a good week," Ellen answered brightly, trying to sound a lot less disappointed than she felt.

Armand saw right through her. "You sound suspiciously like the assortment of hotel clerks who hand me my keys and say, 'Have a good day, sir.' You're not moonlighting, are you?"

"No," she answered with a laugh, knowing she was being teased. She could picture the dark line of his brow and his dark laughing eyes beneath the frown.

"Good. Then say what you're thinking; I'm not a man for beating around the bush. Tell me you'll miss me."

Her heart pounding against her ribs, Ellen kept silent.

"Too much too soon? All right. Well, I will miss you. Everyone else bores me now. Will you at least tell me when your day off is?"

She nodded, drunk with excitement. "Friday *and* Saturday. I must be getting lucky."

"That makes two of us. I'll see you Friday. And Ellen . . . have a good week."

The click of the phone left his husky laughter swirling in her head like smoke. She let the receiver slip from her fingers, scooped her roses into her arms, and waltzed around the living room. Oh, life was wonderful . . . suddenly, unbelievably wonderful! As she danced past the mirror, she caught a glimpse of a young woman with flushed cheeks, her chestnut hair sweeping around her face as she waltzed in time to the music only she could hear. Laughing, she collapsed against the wall and let her heart slow to a gallop. Oh, it was crazy. Crazy and impossible. But it was *happening.* This incredibly wonderful man, this world-famous, suave, debonair conductor was talking to her on the phone about Shosta . . .

Shostakovich? Oh, heavens, she'd have to dig out her old encyclopedia and look up Shostakovich. Maybe she'd better read all the articles on composers. Maybe she'd better go to the library and check out some books! Sign up for a course at the community college . . .

Later!

Dropping into the nearest chair, she buried her face in her roses. The heavy scent acted like a drug: her breathing slowed, her pulse steadied. She'd better put them in water and get some sleep. Everything else would have to wait until she could think clearly again . . . if that ever happened. Closing her eyes, she prayed it never would.

That night at work, at exactly midnight, the emergency room door opened, and instead of another mugging victim, or a kid who had driven his motorcycle into a tree and broken his shoulder, or a man who'd choked on a handful of peanuts in some local bar, in came the florist's delivery boy with his sparkling white ribbon-tied box of roses. Eighteen long-stemmed pink roses exactly the color of sunrise.

Her coworkers were flabbergasted. Was this all for *their* Ellen, the clear-headed, competent, caring but never openly emotional Ellen Farrell they'd worked with for seven years? It didn't seem possible. Why, she didn't even *look* like herself anymore. Oh, the uniform was the same, and she had the same quick, quiet step, the ready hand, even the proper tilt to the starched little white cap. But beneath that cap her eyes shone blue as the sky after a summer rain, and there were spots of bright color high on her cheeks. And when she wasn't with a patient, her thoughts seemed miles away.

They all wondered what was going on, but none wondered as deeply and with such intensity of emotion as did Ellen herself.

At seven-thirty the next morning, before falling into bed after a long night in the hospital, Ellen grabbed her phone and dialed a familiar number.

Her best friend, Laurie Westin, answered the phone with a sleepy yawn. "Hello?"

"Laurie? It's me. Ellen. I've got to talk to you."

"At this hour? Ellen, don't you know expectant mothers are sleeping for two?"

"Sorry," Ellen said, laughing.

"That's okay; I'll pay you back. When the baby wants his two A.M. bottle, I'll tell him to call Aunt Ellen!"

"That's a deal, *if* you can help me figure out what in the world is going on."

Laurie sat up in bed, interested now, while Ellen, on the other end of the line, nervously wound her hair around her fingers.

"Okay, I'm ready."

"Remember I told you about meeting Armand Dante, the conductor? Well, he keeps sending me flowers. And I don't mean a Mother's Day bouquet! I mean roses. Dozens of long-stemmed pink roses. And . . . and Laurie"—she hesitated, her throat tight—"he acts like he really cares for me."

There was a brief silence, and then Laurie's serious, thoughtful voice. "Ellen, that's lovely. You *deserve* roses, and he'd be a fool not to know it; I mean, how many times have Rick and I told you what a gem you are! But Ellen, it sounds like he's really rushing things."

That was not what Ellen had wanted to hear. "What? Look who's talking—one week out of the convent and *you* were head over heels in love with a banjo player!"

Laurie laughed. "Touché, but *he* was irresistible! Is Armand?"

Ellen wanted to shout, Yes, oh, heavens, yes! but she was afraid to risk Laurie's laughter. Instead, she said softly, "He's very, very nice."

"Ellen, I'm not saying he isn't. It's just that he sounds like he, well, lives life in the fast lane. A little out of our class. You understand. . . ." Her voice was full of concern and caring. "I just don't want you to get hurt again."

Ellen clenched her teeth and hid the tremor in her voice. "Of course I understand. You're a real pal for listening. Now go back to bed, and eat well! I want that to be a nice plump baby I'm going to get to hold soon."

"And I'll be glad to let someone else carry him for a change!" Laurie groaned and hung up.

Ellen let the receiver dangle between two fingers, her stomach knotted with a terrible sense of confusion. *She'd been wrong before.* Was she just setting herself up for another disappointment with Armand? Armand! What in the world was she doing getting swept up in some grand passion with a man named *Armand*? Couldn't she just hear her mother's well-intentioned laughter, her father's staunch midwest dismay. Armand? A symphony conductor with a limo and a driver, a sports car, dozens of pink roses, for their plain, sensible little girl? Ha!

But—

But this time *she* wasn't pursuing the relationship, he was! She wasn't trying to please, willing to bend, eager to make concessions and arrangements. No, not this time. And yet he was courting her. Ellen gulped. That *was* what this surprising, magnificent man was doing, wasn't it? Even if she couldn't imagine why!

She dropped the phone back into its cradle and put her roses in water. With uncustomary abandon she drew a hot bath, filled it to the brim with bubbles, and stepped out of her uniform.

"Not bad," she declared, glancing at her image in the steamy mirror. She rubbed her palm over the glass and took another look. "Well, it's not Christie Brinkley, but it's not bad." She was a tall, solid woman, with full breasts, and now she ran her hands over her flat tummy and tight buttocks. What she needed was some pretty lingerie, lace and bows and soft pastel colors. Maybe a sexy nightgown? Maybe . . .

A boisterous chuckle came from her throat, and she dropped her elbows to the vanity top and stared into her own honest blue eyes. Maybe she was jumping the gun here! What she needed was a cold shower, not a hot bath!

But Ellen Farrell never *was* good at taking advice, not even her own. With a toss of her head she gathered her wealth of steam-curled hair up in one hand, knotted it atop her head with a practiced twist of the wrist, and slid languorously into the tub. Her head fell back against the cool tile, her eyelids drooped, and dreams floated behind her lids: Armand's dark eyes, the sweet pressure of his mouth on hers, the perfect, demanding sweep of his arms as he drew exquisite music from the orchestra, all floating on the scent of pink roses.

Later she tried to nap, but for the first time she could remember, sleep eluded her. She tossed and turned, flicked on the radio and flicked it off again, and finally fluffed her pillows and sat in bed reading the paper with the morning sunlight streaming across her bare legs. Turning the pages in the style section, she just glanced at the society gossip column and did a quick double-take.

Our illustrious and oh-so-stylish conductor will be leading the Virginia Youth Symphony Orchestra this week in a performance of Ravel's "Bolero." The only question is, where did Maestro Dante disappear to the evening of Dr. and Mrs. Wellington's elegant-as-always fundraising cocktail party? You have us all breathlessly speculating, Armand . . . what surprises do you have up your coat sleeve this time?

It was several seconds before Ellen realized she had ceased to breathe. Gulping in a huge lungful of air, she steadied herself and carefully, slowly, reread the article. They were wondering about *her*—Ellen Farrell, plain, ordinary Ellen Farrell, nurse, peacemaker, dutiful daughter of John and Helen Farrell. But they didn't know it, of course. Ellen wrapped her arms about herself and shivered. She felt much safer in the warm wrap of anonymity, but slowly the knowledge the such a luxury as privacy was not part of Armand Dante's life began to seep into her confused consciousness.

There was a certain excitement to having some columnist somewhere in a busy newspaper office wondering about her. But when push came to shove, that wasn't Ellen's style . . . no, not at all. Still, the thought of Armand slipping away from the cocktail party to see her slowly pushed all traces of discomfort aside, and with a slow, dreamlike smile, Ellen slipped down between the sheets. In seconds the newspaper slipped forgotten onto the floor, and Ellen drifted off into slumber with sunrises and music and roses . . . and a dark, handsome conductor filling her dreams.

Ellen was on night duty all that week, and each night, at exactly midnight, the roses arrived. And each morning when she got off work, Ellen went home and fell into enough wonderful dreams to last her a lifetime.

By the time the week drew to a close, she was laughingly considering opening up a florist shop with the abundance of roses that overflowed every nook and cranny of her small apartment.

When she left the hospital at seven o'clock that Friday morning, the sky was filled with wind, and white clouds blew across the city like ribbons, or confetti tossed at a parade.

Ellen drove home in a dream. Would he call today? He must; he *must*. Why would he have asked about her days off if he didn't plan to see her? Would the phone be ringing when she got home? Her pulse pounded at her temples, her heart hammered against her ribs. *Nice!* mocked that small, practical inner voice, *look at the state you're in!*

But no amount of deep breathing could still her heart this morning. She knew it was foolish, knew she was asking for trouble, but couldn't do a single sensible thing about it. She was giddy with anticipation. Breathless. Hoping.

She awoke from the dream long enough to find a parking spot near her corner and edged in, congratulating herself. "Lucky day, Farrell!" she said out loud, clutching her box of roses and hurrying up the sidewalk toward her building. Halfway there she almost tripped over her own feet.

Pulled up to the curb at her front door was the gleaming, unmistakable shape of Armand's sports car.

Ellen swallowed around the sudden lump in her throat and continued cautiously up to the car. She peeked inside, squinting to see through the dark-tinted windows; he wasn't there.

She looked around, expecting to see him leaning dramatically against the door, looking wonderfully exotic against the drab brick front, but he wasn't there either. Nor was he standing in the filtered light just inside the swinging doors. And Clarence was nowhere in sight.

Totally baffled, Ellen pushed the door open with her elbow and stepped into the lobby.

"Well, there you are!" Armand's husky baritone sent a jolt of pure electricity surging through her system. He winked. "Another minute and I was going out to search the streets."

Armand was sitting at a wobbly card table behind the doorman's desk, his dark hair falling over one dark brow, his shirt-sleeves rolled up over his forearms. He was holding five playing cards in one hand. From the look on Clarence's face across the table, Armand was winning.

"What—what are you doing here?"

"Waiting for you," came Armand's soft, sexy reply. "I'm taking you to breakfast. Unless you're tired, in which case I shall sit here and play cards with Clarence while you nap. And then we'll call it brunch."

"Oh, lordy, Ms. Farrell, go for *breakfast*! Please! I've lost everything but my socks to this fella of yours."

So they went for breakfast, with just a moment's stop upstairs for Ellen to put her roses in water and slip into a skirt and blouse. From behind the door in the bedroom she could hear Armand moving around her living room, and her hands trembled. If she was having this much trouble just buttoning her blouse, what did the rest of the day hold in store?

Catching her breath, she practiced a quick, self-assured smile in the mirror and stepped into the other room. "Hi. I'm ready."

"And lovely." With that loose, sexy stride of his he crossed the room and took her in his arms. "I've been wanting to do this all week," he whispered, brushing his chin across the silken top of her hair. "Well, *did* you miss me? Just a little maybe?"

She wanted to think of some clever reply, some bright witty remark that he'd remember later and think, Ah, what a chic, clever woman! How irresistible! How sophisticated! Instead, her eyes grew wide, the irises darkening to the color of delphinium petals. "Yes," she said into his shoulder.

"Good! And you liked the flowers?"

Ellen pulled back, laughing. "Liked them?" she repeated incredulously, her gaze sweeping the tiny room that he had transformed into a fairy bower with the extravagant pink blooms. "I love them. They're the most beautiful things I've ever seen!"

His laughter rumbled in his chest. "And *you*, my beauty, are the loveliest thing that *I've* ever seen."

"No, I'm not!" she said without thinking, her honest appraisal leaping to her lips as usual, just one step ahead of her discretion.

"But you are," he answered, stilling her with one finger on her lips. "I could warm my hand in the dark spill of your hair, cool my cheek against the cream of your cheek. I look at you and think, There is someone I want to know. You glow with life. I see a gentle spirit shining through your eyes."

"Stop!" Ellen laughed, pressing her palm to his mouth. "Please, you're embarrassing me." Behind her laughter was the silent thought that she was already lost. She couldn't bear to think that he might not mean what he was saying.

Armand saw the quiver of her pale lips, and his dark eyes narrowed. She didn't believe him. What did she think, that he was some gigolo who handed out such lines as his stock-in-trade? Who needed to? His temper, always too close to the surface, flared briefly, then softened to tenderness. No, what it meant was that someone had hurt her before. Damn! he swore silently, who could have done that to this lovely, precious woman? He felt a swift urge to punch that fool right in the nose!

Armand smiled. He was a man used to getting what he wanted; he had an infinite patience born of success. He'd make everything all right, and enjoy every moment it took. Slow and easy, he cautioned himself, putting a rein on his desire. Slow and easy, and he'd win her heart.

Aloud he said only, "Breakfast?"

Aloud she answered only, "Yes, breakfast."

Five

Armand drove to the Café Galois, where the maître d' bowed formally in greeting and showed them to a single table out on the patio. A striped umbrella cast an island of shade in the bright morning sunlight. There were pink roses on the table. "As you ordered, sir."

"Yes, thank you." Armand nodded with satisfaction. "This will be fine." He turned his dark gaze to Ellen's face and grinned. "It is fine, isn't it, my beauty?"

"It's wonderful," she agreed. "But you don't listen to me! Can't you call me something else?"

"Yes, I could. I could put on a pair of cowboy boots and a ten-gallon hat and call you 'darlin'.' " His grin widened, and mischief flickered in his dark eyes. "Or . . . I could get a crew cut and dig out an old pair of chinos and a button-down shirt and call you 'honey-bunch.' Or I could take you back to my grandfather's home in Salerno and sweep you into my arms in the moonlight on the Mediterranean and call you *'cara mia.'* Choose!"

Her cheeks flaming Ellen stared down at her menu.

Armand had no intention of letting her off so easy. He liked the way the color rose to her face, tinting her pale clear skin with the blush of pink roses. "Well, I await your orders, mademoiselle."

Ellen slid a rueful glance at him and replied, "Eggs Benedict and a cup of black coffee."

With a shout of laughter Armand leaned across the table and kissed the tip of her nose. "I knew there was a reason to get up so early this morning. Ellen, you delight me!"

"You're not so bad yourself, Mr. Dante," she answered.

"*Mister* Dante?" He leaned back, crossing his arms behind his head and stealing Ellen's breath away as the muscles bunched across his broad shoulders. "You know, Ms. Farrell, if I'm not mistaken, you're having a bit of a problem with my name."

"Don't be silly!" Ellen denied, just a little too vehemently. She pressed the back of her hand to her cheek, watching him. "It's just that your name . . . everything about you . . . is so different from anything I've ever known. Exotic. Dramatic. I feel like a schoolgirl who's won a date with a movie star! Or maybe someone's writing a script and I've stumbled onto the set by accident."

"Not accident; no, not even luck. It's fate. Kismet!"

"You really believe that?"

"I didn't one week ago. But today, this morning, yes. I do." He held her eyes, his glance warming her. "So, tell me what name you'd rather call me—Joe? Tom?" He lifted one dark brow. "What were the names of your boyfriends when you were a teenager?"

Ellen chuckled, remembering. "Vinnie. And Lewis. And—" She wrinkled her nose, digging back in time for the memory. "And Bomber!"

"Ah. A tough act to follow!"

"That's not all. There was Salvatore, and Sean and Jo-Jo."

"All those!"

"And that was before I went into the convent."

"Ah, yes, I forgot. But," he teased, "*why* were you in the convent? I can't imagine a more unlikely place for you."

"*Because* of Vinnie and Lewis and Bomber and Salvatore, et cetera." Ellen laughed, thinking fondly of her family. "My parents thought some good, strict discipline might chase the romance out of my foolish head. But as I told you, I lasted only six weeks." Her lovely mouth curved in a grin, and she lifted both shoulders in a little shrug. "And anyway, all it really took was growing up."

"So? Is it gone?"

"Hmmm?" she asked, startled by the sudden intensity of his look, the sensual rasp of his voice.

"The romance. Is it all gone?" he asked, cupping her chin in the palm of his hand.

"I had thought so," Ellen whispered. "Until I met you."

"But a spark is left?" he mused, staring into the lambent depths of her blue eyes. "Yes, I'll stake my life on it! So all it will take is a little practice. Good!" He grinned. He caught hold of her hand and wove his strong fingers between hers. "Then we will begin with my name. Say Armand."

"Armand," Ellen repeated softly, smiling. "Armand. Armand Dante. Armand . . . Armand . . ."

A heady, giddy feeling overtook her, and she pushed back her chair and sauntered across the patio, arms stretched wide, sketching dramatic gestures in the air and fluttering her lashes as she whispered, drawled, sang his name. In moments she had him laughing out loud. Elbow propped on the arm of his chair, he watched her intently, his dark eyes shining. "You are always a surprise, Ellen." He shook his head, hiding his grin behind his hand.

"Yes, Armand?" she practiced teasingly. "Oh, Armand . . . but of course, Armand!" Spinning, she flung her arms wide and hit the waiter right in the stomach.

"Ooomph. You wanted something, madam?"

"Oh, I'm so sorry! No, I—I was just practicing uh . . . something for a play."

"Well, I am sure madam will be a knockout." Without any change of expression he rubbed his stomach and disappeared.

Armand and Ellen broke into gales of laughter. When they could finally catch their breath, Armand reached over and pushed the hair back from her face, tucking it behind the shell of her ear. He held his palm pressed against the curve of her cheek, smiling.

"I think we must practice more quietly."

"Yes." She smiled, loving the feel of his hand against her skin. "Yes, we must."

"For example," he said, smiling into her eyes, "I

could say, 'Isn't it a beautiful morning?' and you would say—"

"Yes, it is, Armand."

"Ah, a fast learner," he whispered, stroking his fingertips across her cheekbone. "And then I could say, 'And isn't this a lovely place to spend a beautiful morning?' "

"Yes, it is, Armand."

"And does being here together make you as happy as it makes me?"

"Yes, Armand."

"And . . ." His fingers tightened in her hair, drawing her closer even as he rose and leaned toward her. His breath was warm on her lips. "Shall I kiss you?"

"Yes, Armand."

She felt the pressure of his mouth, its passionate demand. His lips clung to hers with bruising sweetness, and her head was filled with the scent of his cologne mingled with the heat of his body. Her whole body tightened, aching with overwhelming desire.

She parted her lips to let the tip of her tongue touch his. He tasted sweeter than any forbidden fruit, sweeter and more intoxicating than any nectar of the gods. Her head spun; her knees wobbled. She wrapped her arms around his neck, wanting him, willing this kiss to last forever.

If it had been up to Armand, it would have!

He was on fire with the taste of her, the cool sweetness of her mouth. Her scent filled his head, and the brush of her thick silken hair against his face aroused him still more. He wanted her. He felt the hot surge of desire and his kiss deepened, his mouth hungering for her. . . .

"Ahem." The waiter announced his approach discreetly.

Ellen and Armand tore themselves apart, staggering, dropping heavily into the two chairs on opposite sides of the table.

Ellen pressed her open hand against her heaving chest, struggling to catch her breath.

Armand rigidly gripped the arms of his chair, looking like a man struck by lightning.

The waiter approached.

"Are you ready to order, sir?"

"I—I think so." He frowned across the table, his eyes focusing only on Ellen's blushing face. "Uh . . . what meal is this?" he whispered sotto voce.

"Breakfast. I think we're supposed to be having breakfast," she replied with great seriousness, and then they both began to laugh.

Sunday's society column held this bit of news:

Guess whom we saw breakfasting at Café Galois last Friday morning! And here we thought our illustrious and oh-so-eligible symphony conductor was devoting all of his time to his performances. *Not* that we've ever known his performance to be anything but perfect . . . both at the podium, and *elsewhere.* But we are just dying to know, Armand, who *was* your mysterious and lovely breakfast companion?

Ellen felt a chill walk up her spine. There it was again—her life being looked at by strangers. A dozen feelings swelled up in her as she leaned back against the pillows of her bed. She felt frightened, exposed. But at the same time the clipping underlined the wondrous excitement that was weaving itself into the fabric of her life because of one man, Armand Dante.

She did feel mysterious and lovely, she had to admit. Mysterious . . . and lovely . . . and in love. The whole weekend had been heavenly. They'd spent every waking moment together, and she had dreamed of him each night. By some unspoken agreement they had both gone back to their own homes, their own beds at night, and there was a certain sweetness in their abstinence. Perhaps the sweetness was in the anticipation, knowing as they both did that they would make love . . . when the time was right.

Six

"If he's so terrific, Ellen, why are you keeping him hidden? From your best friends, no less!"

"Hidden!" she echoed over the phone, laughing with disbelief. She flopped down on her bed and kicked off her crepe-soled nurses' shoes. "Are you kidding? The only thing about this relationship that's driving me crazy is that I *can't* keep him hidden. Not one moment just to ourselves. Every time I open the morning paper, there it is, a blow-by-blow description of everything we've done in the last twenty-four hours! What I'd really love to do is steal him away, have him all to myself. Oh, Laurie"—her voice dropped to a trembling whisper—"he's so wonderful. So dashing and gallant and . . . *incredible*, he takes my breath away! I can't believe I'm this lucky."

"Maybe he's the lucky one," came Laurie's stubborn, loyal reply. "Maybe, like Rick, he got tired of all the hoopla, the publicity and the demands . . ."

"The standing ovations, and the glamorous women waiting backstage, and the cocktail parties and European concerts? Sure!"

"Well, did you ever think what a refreshing change you must be after all that?"

"Yup! Like taking the métro after too many flights on a Concorde," Ellen tossed back with a laugh.

"I'm not joking," Laurie scolded. "You are a wonderful person. Honest and forthright—"

"Painfully blunt?"

"No. Candid and open-hearted. Constant as the north star. And loving."

"Oh, I'm loving all right. So much at the moment that it scares me."

Laurie had been waiting for just that admission. Sounding just a tiny bit like her mother superior back in the convent, she cautioned, "Is that wise, Ellen? Are you sure he cares about you the same way?"

"Yes." Ellen smiled to herself in the empty room.

"How do you know?"

"Because he tells me so."

She said it with irrefutable conviction, remembering the touch of his fingertips on her face, the sudden smile lighting his dark eyes, the tenderness in his husky voice. He seemed as surprised as she by this quirk of fate. Surprised and delighted. He would kiss her, pull back to study her face, and then, smiling, lower his mouth to hers again. She could taste him now.

Grinning, Ellen grabbed a pillow and hugged it to her chest. "Laurie, I've got to go now. You called just as I walked in the door, and if I don't get out of this uniform, I'm going to scream."

"Just hold your horses. Besides, don't you know you're not allowed to scream at a pregnant woman? Ellen, your bedside manner has gone to pot during this romance!"

"That's because I haven't practiced my bed*room* manner—and my dreams are running me ragged!"

"What?" Laurie's gasp of embarrassment quickly shifted to surprise. "Oh, I just assumed . . . I mean, he *is* Armand Dante. A bit of notoriety goes with that name!"

"I must have been the only person on the East Coast who didn't know that." Ellen sighed.

"Well," came Laurie's pronouncement, "I must say I like him a bit better now. Which gets me back to why I called in the first place."

"Finally!"

"Rick's saved our table at the theater tonight. Say you and Armand will come, please! We're dying to meet him, and we miss you terribly. At eight?"

"I'll have to ask Armand, but I think it'll be fine. He doesn't have a performance tonight—"

"I know. I checked."

Ellen laughed fondly. "You're impossible! See you at eight."

"You're *sure* you don't mind, Armand?" Ellen asked for the third time as he wove his sports car in and out of traffic on the way to the Stage Theater.

He lifted one hand from the steering wheel and slipped it beneath the hair at the nape of her neck, tugging playfully at the silky strands. "I'm happy to meet your friends, Ellen. And seeing Rick Westin perform is always a pleasure. I'm only hoping I pass muster." He shot her a sideways teasing glance, his dark eyes flashing. "Will you throw me over if they don't approve?"

"How could they not approve?" She laughed, catching his hand between her shoulder and cheek. His hand was cool, but her cheek was warm and flushed, soft and yielding as a ripe peach.

Armand felt his heart hammer against the wall of his chest. That had never happened before, not with any other woman, and it still caught him by surprise. Narrowing his eyes, he quickly glanced from the traffic back to her upturned face.

"You look at me in a different way than anyone ever has." He licked his dry lips and continued in a low, husky voice. "Ellen, there *are* those who don't approve of me. Oh, they may want something, demand something, need something from me because of my talent, my fame, my reputation"— his lip curled in a hint of a sneer—"so they hide their resentment behind smiles and handshakes, but they're transparent. And then, well, there are those who approve *too* easily; my reputation has already bought their good opinion, and they couldn't tell my best performance from my worst."

Curling her legs up under her on the leather seat, Ellen stared at his perfect profile, and for a moment he was a stranger, a photo in some glossy magazine. Cold and hard as ice. She couldn't stand it, and pressed her hand against the side of his face, wanting and giving at the same time.

His chest rose, making his starched shirt crinkle, and she heard his sharply indrawn breath. "Ellen," he whispered, and turned to her, a smile lighting the smoky depths of his dark eyes. "Tell me, what do you see when you look at me like that?"

"I see a man who doesn't seem to know how perfectly wonderful he is. I see a man so blazing with passion that everyone else fades in comparison."

"Not everyone," he corrected her gently, turning his face to kiss her palm. "You shine."

"I'm afraid, my good sir," she said, blushing, "that's just reflected light."

"Nonsense. It comes from some deep well within you, rising up in your eyes, spilling over your lovely face. You know some secret I'll never learn. But you make me want to learn it, share it. I'll tell you something, Ellen—" He paused, raked his fingers through his dark hair, and shook his head. "I don't conduct well when I know you're watching."

"I . . . I'll stop coming!"

"Don't you dare! No, you unnerve me, throw me off balance. My timing, my commands seem— what?—polished and dramatic, but inadequate knowing that you are out there, experiencing the music through me. I had grown so used to acclaim, I was bored by it. But you make me want to be better than I am."

"Impossible. You're perfect."

Ignoring his pleased, boyish laugh, she slid her fingers down inside the collar of his shirt, enjoying the touch of his unseen skin, imagining the rest of him, all warm and hard and smooth.

His breath hissed between clenched teeth. "That's taking unfair advantage. Remind me never to buy a stick shift again!" Throwing the car into the next gear, he freed his right hand and slid it up the length of her leg, his fingers cupping the warm flesh of her thigh through her silk skirt.

Ellen giggled. "Stop that! I feel like a teenager on my first date."

"Good. Then let's ditch your friends and go park somewhere. We can make out in the back seat."

"This car doesn't *have* a back seat!" She laughed, her head spinning with the delicious promise of his touch.

"Fine! Then I'll take you to our special sunrise place, and I'll throw my jacket on the ground and pull you down on top of me and we'll make sweet, endless love."

Ellen closed her eyes and drew a shallow, trembling breath. She could feel herself melting at just the sound of his voice, the promise of his words. This was terrible! Edging to the far side of her bucket seat, she crossed her legs and dug her nails into her palms. Count to ten! she ordered herself silently, but she had only gotten to two when his voice sent fresh waves of desire washing through her.

"Ellen? Don't you want me as much as I want you?"

"Oh, lordy!" she gasped without thinking. "That's like asking Cinderella if she'd like to dance with the prince!"

"Ellen!" With a groan of muffled laughter he smacked the heel of his hand against his forehead. "You do know how to defuse a moment. Now, cut that out; I'm no prince!"

Ellen stared across the dim interior of the car at Armand. She was looking at him with eyes that had seen too much: years of a nurse's reality of pain, sadness, and disillusionment. But now, as she rested her chin on the back of her hand and smiled at him, her eyes were shining. "Listen to me, Armand Dante. I'm just an ordinary woman. Plain vanilla. But I am an expert romantic. And you are pure fantasy."

He didn't answer. The Stage Theater loomed ahead, and he maneuvered the car into a parking space, stepped out, and came around to open her door without saying a word. His dark brows were drawn in a fierce line, and his bronze skin was stretched taut across his jaw. He took her hand and drew her out of the car, then caught her to him with one arm around her waist. His broad hand pressed flat against the small of her back, and she could feel his heat and power. "But what if I can't live up to your fantasy?"

"Oh, Armand," she said in a tiny voice, her knees buckling. "You've already surpassed it!"

Laurie was waiting for them in the lobby, looking very pregnant in a navy and white striped maternity dress. And even as she was enveloped in Ellen's bear hug of welcome, her wide, appraising eyes were on Armand.

"Mr. Dante, how nice to meet you," she said, extending her hand.

Armand heard the hint of reserve in her voice and felt a swift stab of annoyance. Judged already, was he? For an instant he was tempted to click his heels together and offer a small courtly bow, perhaps even kiss the back of her hand, but he resisted, biting back his grin so that all that gave him away was a rueful glint in his dark eyes. He would not tease, not mock . . . not tonight. If tonight was important to Ellen, he'd behave.

"I'm very glad to meet you also, Laurie." He

smiled, taking her hand. "And it's always a pleasure to hear your husband perform. I'm looking forward to meeting him."

Releasing her hand, he slipped his arm around Ellen's warm, slender waist, letting his hand rest familiarly on the curve of her hip. She felt wonderful, tall and big-boned, a good match for his long, lean body. He wanted to press his face in her hair, nibble on the soft pad of her earlobe. Instead, he smiled coolly. "Shall we go in?"

Rick Westin was already on the stage, tuning the last of his five banjos, tapping his foot, and telling a joke to a table full of tourists from Wyoming, all at the same time. When he saw his wife, his grin widened and he jumped down off the stage. "Hi, darlin'; hi, baby!" He grinned, patting Laurie's stomach and making her blush. He wrapped Ellen in a hug of welcome and stuck out his hand.

"Hey, it's great to meet you, Armand. We've missed Ellen and figured there had to be something mighty special keeping her away."

"Thanks, Rick. But *she's* the something special!"

"Enough, you two!" Ellen broke in, feeling the heat rise to her cheeks. "The Ellen Farrell fan club will reconvene after the show. Refreshments will be served. Right now, don't you have a show to put on, Westin?"

Rick Westin put on one heck of a show. Used to the spotlight himself, Armand knew nothing was as easy as Rick made it look. He watched with a showman's eye, enjoying the relaxed exuberance of the man's performance, comparing it to the

strained tension and passion of his own con-
ducting. How different it was to hear the hearty
laughter of the audience and their whistles and
applause when what he himself knew was the
great silence of the symphony hall, the awesome
swell of music drawn out by his baton, and then
the resounding thunder of applause.

He glanced over at Ellen, wanting to know what
she was thinking. He wished desperately that he
knew her well enough to be able to read her
thoughts from the lively play of expressions across
her face. He wanted to know her so well that he
could slip inside her skin and feel the racing of her
heart, the heat of her blood.

When Rick began his final song, the lights
dimmed and he sat on the edge of the stage looking
into Laurie's eyes as he sang.

Ellen sat pressed against the back of her chair,
watching, moved as always by the beauty of the
moment.

Armand watched only her. In the soft glow of the
single spotlight he could see her eyes glisten with
tears. His stomach twisted. He wanted to do that!
He wanted to be the only one who could bring tears
to her eyes, his the only music that would make
her weep. Jealousy mixed with a fierce resolve shot
through him.

The sudden rise of the houselights caught them
both unprepared. Ellen hastily brushed her
fingertips across her cheeks, and Armand drew his
usual cool composure back in place like a shield.
Laurie had abandoned them, going to lean against
Rick's knee as he chatted happily with the
departing audience, and their table was a tiny
island of silence in the noisy room.

"Well, what did you think?" Ellen asked finally. "I know, you must think I'm crazy, but things like that always get to me. I cry at 'The Star Spangled Banner,' and the circus when the tightrope walker makes it all the way across and the crowd cheers, and during every rerun of *Little House on the Prairie*. I—I don't know, I'm just a sucker for shmaltz! And never take me to old Tracy-Hepburn movies; I'd embarrass you to death!"

Armand caught her hand in his, weaving their fingers together. "You could never embarrass me, Ellen. And I want to take you everywhere, every-place you've ever dreamed of . . . places you've never imagined!" His voice was rough-edged. "Just the two of us, Ellen, on a private island in the Medi-terranean, perhaps! With no public, no newspa-pers, no—"

"Hey, you two, let's go get a pizza!" Rick boomed, dropping a hand on each of their shoulders.

Armand held her gaze for just a fraction of a sec-ond longer, then released her, hiding his impa-tience behind a friendly smile. But Ellen saw that flicker in his ebony eyes and felt a sudden thrill of excitement. He really *did* want her, and all this, the evening with friends, the light conversation, these things that had previously satisfied her, now were only a prelude to something more. She didn't dare name it, not yet.

As they left the theater, a flashbulb popped, and a woman's brash voice exclaimed, "It *is* you— Armand Dante—right? Sure, I told my husband it was; we saw you last fall at the Kennedy Center and thought you were terrific. Only time I ever liked classical music. Do ya think I could have a picture of you and Rick Westin together? The girls in my Mah-Jongg group would love it!"

"Not tonight. I'm sorry."

"Oh, please!" the woman begged, already aiming the camera at the two men.

Rick shrugged, threw an arm around Armand's shoulder, and flashed a grin. Beside him Armand stood grim-faced. The woman never noticed, just took her picture and departed with a wave, her heels sounding like gunshots in the dark.

Rick laughed. "Whew! Does that happen often?"

"More often than I like." Armand groaned, rolling his shoulders to ease the tension in his muscles. He shook his dark head. "I suppose I should be more gracious; at least she found she liked classical music."

"I have a feeling she liked seeing you wave your baton more than she liked Mozart!"

"I know. That's what infuriates me, that and the damned rudeness—"

"Whoa, fellas!" Ellen slipped in between the two men, her eyes blazing. "You two picked your professions, and I know *one* someone who sure enjoys his Georgetown address, and *another* someone who seems to have no trouble zipping around in his luxury sports car when he's not being chauffeured in his limo. You should be kinder to your public!"

"Ah, champion of the abused and misunderstood!" Rick quipped. "I'd forgotten about that temper of yours, kiddo."

"And I've never seen it before." Armand grinned, folding his arms across his broad chest.

"That's because you've had me under some kind

of spell, Mr. Dante. But stick around, and you're sure to find out all kinds of things about me."

"I intend to do just that," Armand answered, brushing his lips across her brow.

Her frown vanished. "Oh, how do you do what you do to me?" she whispered so that only he could hear.

"Stick around and you're sure to find out."

Ellen never even tasted the pizza; she hardly heard the banter of conversation around the Westins' kitchen table. Her whole being was focused on Armand's coal-black eyes, and the promise she saw glowing there. A river of desire flowed through her veins. Her skin seemed unusually sensitive; the breeze from the window, the brush of his jacket sleeve, excited her. When he took off his jacket and rolled his shirt-sleeves to the elbow, baring his bronze skin, her fingertips seemed drawn as to some powerful magnet. Helplessly she placed her hand on his arm, and he turned in the middle of a sentence and smiled at her. Did he know? Did he know what power he had over her?

The clock ticked off the minutes, and just when she thought she couldn't wait any longer, thought she'd explode with waiting and wanting, Armand stood and held his hand out to her. "Think we should be going?" His voice was all silken casualness, but his eyes flashed. Did he know? Did he know she'd been counting the minutes, willing the clock hand forward?

"Maybe we'd better." She smiled sweetly, adding, "Laurie needs her rest." She couldn't believe her voice could sound so steady, so cool, when her whole body was on fire.

They said good night to Laurie and Rick and hurried out to Armand's car. He held the door open, careful not to touch her as she slid into the seat. But he smiled a sensual, knowing smile full of desire and anticipation. Ellen drew a shaky breath through her parted lips. She tried to sit still, hands folded in her lap as the car drove down the dark street, but she couldn't. She turned in her seat, gathered her legs up under her, and rested her cheek against the back of her seat. "Armand?"

"Yes?"

She blushed. "Nothing. I—I just wanted to say your name."

He reached over and drew one finger slowly across her lips. "I want more than that. I want to hear you call my name in the night. I want to hold you in my arms until sunrise and love you all through the day. I want your face to be the first thing I see when I open my eyes."

"Oh, Armand . . ." Her voice gave a little wobble and vanished.

"There's nothing to be afraid of, love. Trust me."

In moments he had parked beneath the elegant old apartment building where he lived. Holding her hand, he led her to the elevator and pushed the button marked Nine. There wasn't one for ten, but then the numbers resumed.

"Oops, someone swiped the floor above you," Ellen joked through chattering teeth, needing to ease the incredible tension between them.

"No, love," Armand answered, a small smile tugging at the corners of his mouth. "I have both floors."

"You what?" Ellen blinked, thinking of her third floor walkup.

"Now, don't get skittish on me. You know who I am. And you said yourself I enjoy the perks of the job. Now I want you to enjoy them with me; I want to throw them at your feet."

"And I can tromp on them with my crepe soles!"

"Then I shall buy you satin slippers!" He laughed, pulling her closer and closer still until her breasts were flattened against the hard wall of his chest and her breath was on his lips. He held her like that for a full moment, his eyes caressing her face, and then he lowered his mouth to hers and kissed her so passionately, her bones felt as if they would melt. There was nothing holding her to earth but the hot, fierce press of his lips.

Ellen squeezed her eyes shut and rose up on tiptoe, wrapping her arms around his neck and kissing him back hungrily. She was aware of nothing but their mouths clinging and parting, turning and pressing, one mouth against the other like pieces of a puzzle that fit perfectly together. Armand lifted his head slightly, savoring the sweet torture of that inch of empty space dividing them, and then recaptured her mouth with almost bruising desire. He nipped the full curve of her bottom lip, slid his tongue into the velvet recesses of her mouth. A groan rumbled in his throat, sending shivers racing across her skin. And deep within her Ellen felt her passion flame and rise, forcing her to cling to him because there was nothing else on earth but him.

The elevator door slid open, startling them both.

Gasping and laughing, drunk on the taste of each other, they stumbled out of the elevator. Armand fished a key from his pocket, but couldn't fit it into the lock; he was too busy burying his face in the chestnut fall of her hair, nibbling at the nape of her neck, slipping his tongue into the curve of her ear.

"Stop . . . oh, stop," she moaned, tangling her hands in the thick mane of his dark hair. "Armand! Oh, I love you . . . love you. Oh, stop . . ."

"Never!"

One flick of his wrist and the door swung open. "Ready?" He laughed, a low husky sound that matched his dark, smoldering gaze. Then he scooped her up in his arms and carried her inside, kicked the door shut, strode up a circular staircase, and into his bedroom.

"Wait! Oh, what a gorgeous apartment!" Ellen cried, squirming in his arms. "That view . . . the furniture! . . . and you stole the staircase from some fairy-tale castle, I know it!"

"Hush, woman. You get the ten-dollar tour later."

"But—"

"Nothing but *this*," he growled, kissing her more fiercely than he had before, drawing a response from the very heart of her. She caressed his face, his neck, the bunched muscles in his shoulders, the broad, smooth plane of his upper back. But that was all she could reach. Suddenly she had to know the angle of his hips, the hard curve of his buttocks, the rock-hard muscles in his tensed thighs. Her hands, her whole body, ached for the feel of him.

"Put me down! Put me down!"

He did, but held her tight within the circle of his arms.

"What?" he gasped, his chest heaving. He was balanced on the very edge of self-control, wanting to grab her and throw her on the bed. He was burning, and he drew harsh breaths as though to bank the fire until he could be sure she was ready. "What is it, love?" He groaned softly, afraid to hear her answer.

Ellen blushed furiously, the color staining her cheeks and neck. "I—I wanted to be able to touch you, hold you. I couldn't reach and . . ."

With a whoop of joy Armand took her in his arms and fell with her onto the wide bed. "Oh, my darling, darling Ellen, there's never been anyone like you. Never! You delight me!"

"You're not so bad yourself!" She laughed giddily, stretching against the length of him, her hands stroking his chest and ribs through his clothes. His heart pounded beneath her palm and his once starched white shirt was limp from the heat of his body. Her own heart beat to the same mad rhythm, sending tremors through her aching flesh.

As if he felt that same trembling arousal, his hand cupped her breast; his thumb circled her nipple, caressing first one breast and then the other, his palm rubbing the silk of her dress against her until the heat of his hand and the slide of the silk became unbearably erotic.

She whimpered, and he lifted himself on one elbow and leaned over her, his dark eyes glazed with desire. He bent to kiss her mouth, her throat, the hollow of her shoulder. She caught his head in her hands and brought his lips back to hers, sliding her tongue across his beautifully chiseled mouth. And suddenly they were tumbling across the bed, their arms and legs tangled together.

Just as suddenly Armand tore himself away and knelt, straddling her hips with his hard thighs. He was grinning and panting at the same time, his eyes blazing. "Shall we get more comfortable?"

Ellen gave a shaky, breathless laugh. "Most definitely!" she whispered, shuddering with pleasure as his hands moved down the row of buttons on her nearly destroyed silk dress. He opened each button slowly, and parted the fabric bit by bit as he went.

Trembling, she began to undo the top button of his shirt, but by the time he reached her waist, she was still struggling with that first impossible button. "Oh, what the hell—" She groaned, grabbed both sides of his shirt, and ripped the buttons right off.

With a shout of surprise and excitement Armand peeled off her dress. He bent his dark head to kiss her breasts and stomach through her silk teddy, and Ellen pulled his shirt down over his shoulders and arms, tugging the tails out of his slacks as he dropped his weight across her.

They kissed, nipping at each other's lips, the tiny jolts of pain fueling their excitement. There were no words, just soft love moans and cries of passion.

Wild with desire, Ellen rolled out from beneath him and unfastened the buckle of his belt. She laid her trembling hand on the zipper of his slacks, and Armand caught her palm, pressing it against the surging, aching heat of his arousal. He tore off his pants and briefs and kicked them to the floor. He was naked, hard and glistening with sweat, kneeling over her like some god, and the power and perfection of him made her gasp.

"Oh, you are the most . . . most beautiful man I've ever seen!"

He laughed, shaking his head, his eyes blazing, his lips parted. "Ellen, love, it's you who are beautiful." He kissed her shoulder, slipping off one thin lace strap. "Exquisite." He kissed the other shoulder. "Bewitching." The teddy joined the pile of discarded clothing on the floor. His gaze softened, traveling slowly over her nakedness. "I will teach you to know how beautiful you are," he whispered.

Ignoring her soft little cries, he brushed his lips across the pale rise of her breasts. "You're like fresh cream." His tongue swept in wet, hot circles across her nipples as she writhed and moaned. "Sweet as strawberries, love." His mouth drew a hot trail down to her quivering belly. "Honey," he whispered, reckless now with the pleasure of loving her, tasting her, touching her. But his words became a groan as Ellen slid down beneath him and wrapped her legs around his hips.

"Armand . . . Armand, love me now," she begged, trembling, pierced through with an ecstasy that was almost pain. One moment, one touch more and she would shatter into a thousand pieces. She clung to him tighter, pressing against his strong body, whispering his name over and over against his lips, his hair, his brow, hardly aware of what her passion was doing to him until she heard the harsh cry torn from his throat.

"Yes, love, my love," he groaned, past all restraint now, desire thrusting through his body like a blade. And with his mouth and hands and body he took her, making her his own, giving himself completely to her.

It was as if this were the first time for both of them. And like the sweeping power of his music, they were the two strains of a melody uniting, rising, soaring to a perfect heart-stopping crescendo.

Later in the dark she stirred and called his name and he woke and gathered her to him, rubbing his cheek against her breasts and stroking the insides of her thighs until they were both wild again. They made love first on the bed and then on the thick fuzzy rug on the floor. That was where they slept finally, with the quilt yanked half off the bed for cover, and her head pillowed on his shoulder.

When Ellen woke, the buttercup light of morning was spilling through the bedroom windows. She opened one eye, then both, surprised to find herself back in Armand's wide bed, and alone.

Swinging her feet over the side of the bed, Ellen pushed her tousled cinnamon-colored hair out of her eyes and found a thick terry robe draped over the foot of the bed. Slippers waited beside her bare feet. A single rose lay across the other pillow. Happiness filled her like helium in a rainbow-colored balloon, and she floated out of bed and down the hall to the top of the staircase.

There was music coming from downstairs. It took only a moment to realize it was no record or radio, but Armand playing the piano. He was practicing, playing some intricate set of exercises or scales over and over, tirelessly, perfectly. She slipped silently down the stairs, and perched on a low step, her arms wrapped around her knees.

The room was spare, done in white, and the eye was drawn first to the grand piano placed in the center of a Persian rug. It was magnificent, all dark and shining, and so was the man seated on the bench, his head bent in fierce concentration. Armand filled the pale room with his incredible presence. Despite his casual chinos and knit shirt, he looked grand, beautiful. He was the most handsome man she had ever seen. It seemed impossible that she had just spent the night with him. Impossible that he loved her. Impossible to love anyone as much as she knew she loved him!

When he looked up suddenly and smiled, her heart stopped. His smile said everything: He did love her; this was not just a dream.

"Good morning, my beauty. Did I wake you?"

"I missed you. I couldn't bear the empty space where you had been."

"Good." That one word was enough. He looked deep into her eyes, then placed his hands back on the keys and said softly, "I have a present for you."

He played Chopin's "Fantaisie-Impromptu" for her alone. It was magical—as sensual and seductive as his lovemaking. Ellen felt the music move through her, heightening her senses, binding her to him. She watched his hands on the keys, his mane of dark hair, his arrogant, handsome face and blazing, passionate eyes, and knew she loved him beyond thought or reason. This was the one man she would love forever.

When he stopped, she had to press her hands to her lips to keep from crying.

He came and lifted her in his arms, thinking he would carry her back up to the bedroom, but she was already kissing his eyes, his mouth, and he knew he'd never make it back up those stairs.

A sound, half-laugh, half-groan, rose to his throat, and he felt his heart pound, his knees buckle. How could she do this to him? Just a glance at her tangled hair, the pale rise of her breasts inside his old terry robe, and he was burning with desire. Just the musky scent of her sleep-warm skin, and his body tightened into an arousal so powerful it was painful. He stumbled to an over-stuffed armchair and they fell into it, laughing, already loving each other.

Seven

The autumn days flew by on a wave of happiness Ellen had never dreamed possible. Away from Armand life was wonderful, experienced through eyes dazzled by his image and a heart that overflowed with love. And with Armand life was exquisite.

One perfect Sunday morning they were munching croissants and dropping crumbs in their laps as they read the morning paper. Suddenly Armand groaned. "Oh, damn!"

Ellen leaned over and planted a marmalade kiss on his lips. "What's the matter?" she asked, snuggling closer to his warm bare flank.

Scowling, he folded the page and tossed it to the floor on his side of the bed. "It's nothing! Just that damn gossip column again. I get sick and tired of their intruding on my private life. *Our* life! Speculations, innuendos—"

"I know, Armand." She rested her chin on his knee. Her blue eyes clouded with frustration, but their steady gaze never wavered. "I know; I hate it too."

"You do, don't you? Oh, Ellen, I'll do something about it; I'll make it stop! I'll—"

"Shhh, love," she whispered, pushing his dark hair back from his furrowed brow. "It's just nonsense; you always tell *me* not to pay any attention. Here, let's see what they've come up with now." She leaned over his legs, her breasts brushing against the dark hair on his thighs, laughing huskily as she scooped up the paper. "Now, what did they say that got you so upset?"

"No!" Armand tried to take the paper from her hands. "It's nothing. You're right. I don't know why I bother to read it."

But Ellen had already pressed the paper over her legs and was curiously scanning the columns.

She gasped, too surprised to hide her initial shock.

There was a picture of her, taken years before, when she graduated from nursing school. Her hair was tied back in a bun beneath her starched cap, her uniform made her look as shapeless as a schoolgirl, and her huge eyes seemed to fill her pale face. She looked like someone's maiden aunt. The caption read:

Is this what's keeping our illustrious conductor under covers these days?

Before she could stop them, tears welled in her eyes and spilled down her face.

"Love, oh, love, don't cry. Please," Armand

begged, crouching on his knees before her and wiping her face with his hands. "No . . . don't cry! It's nothing to cry about."

"But it is, Armand. It is! Don't you see?" She stopped, unable to explain. Her emotions were so confused, so muddled, she could hardly understand them herself. "I—I look so ridiculous," was all she could finally whisper.

"You do not!" he shouted, suddenly almost as angry with her as he was with the column. "You look sweet, and serious, and dedicated. You look like a young girl with an ideal that glows inside her like a candle. You look beautiful, and if I had seen that picture, I would have had it framed and hung over the mantel!"

"Oh, Armand, you are crazy . . . crazy and wonderful." She wrapped her arms around his neck as her tears ran slowly down her cheeks. "But it makes me so angry, Armand. They have no right!" She rubbed her head gently against his shoulder.

"No, my love, they don't. They just think they do because of who I am. But it doesn't matter, don't you see? Not unless we let it. It doesn't matter at all as long as you trust me, not them or the foolish way they try to play with other people's lives."

Armand reached for the paper and looked again at the old photo, a slow smile spreading from his eyes to his lips. He stroked her hair gently and whispered softly into her ear, "Besides, it really is lovely, you know." He kissed her on the tip of her nose. "Just as you are, my beauty. I could never want anyone else, Ellen. It's you I love."

Ellen kissed him back. "And I love you."

"No more worries? No more tears?" he prompted

her, his playful, tender kisses punctuating his words.

"No, I promise!" She laughed, wiggling beneath the sweet teasing of his lips on her throat and breasts. "Armand," she said breathlessly, "what *are* you doing?"

And then she forgot everything but the wonder of loving this incredible man.

"Ellie, I need sunshades when you come in here these days. May I be so presumptuous as to say that classical music agrees with you?" Elliott Rosen slid his glasses down over his large nose and peered over them at his favorite nurse. The gradual weakening of the aging playwright's body had done nothing to dull his mind, and he was following the gradual change in Ellen Farrell with both amusement and delight.

Ellen beamed. "Agrees, fulfills, moves me into another world, Mr. Rosen."

"Dvorak, you mean." The old man's eyes twinkled as he watched her.

Ellen reached for his wrist and wrapped her fingers expertly around it, then looked down at her watch. "Certainly, Dvorak, Mr. Rosen. What else could I possibly mean?"

"What I want to know is when I'm going to meet the 'what else you could possibly mean,' " he teased. "When are you going to bring the esteemed maestro by? I won't be around forever, you know. And gossip has it that he's no stranger to this hospital."

Ellen looked at him softly without answering, an idea taking hold in her mind. In recent days the

whole staff had noticed that Elliott Rosen's pro-
longed hospital stay was beginning to weary his
spirit, and Ellen decided she had just the right
medicine.

It was after visiting hours the next night, and
shortly after the conclusion of the symphony concert, when Armand Dante, elegantly dressed in
casual slacks and a handsome blue V-neck
sweater, moved stealthily down the hall to Elliott
Rosen's hospital room. Ellen was waiting at the
door, an excited smile on her face.

"Shhh, Armand," she whispered as he swept her
off her feet and kissed her lovingly on the lips.

"What's the matter, my beauty? Don't all the vis-
itors greet you this way?" He rubbed his finger
gently down the side of her cheek, unwilling to let
her slip away.

"Of course, Armand. But it's after hours, you
see, and—"

As he stopped her words with another kiss,
Armand slipped his arm around her back and
pressed her close. "We've been apart far too long,
my love."

"Yes, approximately three hours, I believe,
since you rushed in and out on your way to the
concert."

Armand's deep, rumbling laugh echoed in the
quiet, well-lit hall. "You think I'm foolish, do you?
Well, I'll show you—"

Before he could kiss her again, Ellen slipped out
of his arms and put her hand on the large metal
door handle. "We should go in before he falls
asleep. Come on!"

Armand nodded and followed her quietly into the room.

"Mr. Rosen, are you awake?" Ellen asked softly.

"If I wasn't before, I am now," the old man retorted. "You want I should get out of bed to see you? Come on in here, Ellie, and stop sneaking around in the shadows." He fumbled on the bedside table for his glasses.

"Mr. Rosen, I brought a friend to see you, but you have to keep your voice down because it's late, and we'll all get in trouble if we're overheard."

Elliott Rosen lifted himself up on one elbow as Ellen drew Armand over to the bed.

"Mr. Rosen, I'd like you to meet a friend of mine. Armand Dante, Elliott Rosen."

Elliott stuck his glasses on his nose and stared at the man standing in front of him.

"Hello, Mr. Rosen. Ellen has told me so much about you."

"About me?" he croaked. "Well, I'll be damned! You sit right down there on the edge of the bed, Maestro, and don't you move an inch. Well, well. Well, I'll be damned." He didn't turn his head, but managed to throw a few words in Ellen's direction. "You know, I was kidding you, Ellie. About your bringing him in here. But I want to tell you this— it's an honor to be sure."

"The honor is mine, Mr. Rosen. Ellen tells me you're the one who taught her how to listen to my music. I came to thank you for that."

Elliott's wrinkled face glowed beneath the praise.

"And there's something else—"

Elliott leaned forward in the bed, determined not to miss a single word.

"I saw one of your plays, *Song of Sixpence*, when

the Virginia Repertory did it last year, and I think the second act was a stroke of genius! It's a wonderful play."

Ellen watched the two men for a moment as they admired the artist in each other. She saw the old man's face brighten with a vitality she hadn't seen there before, and then she slipped unnoticed out the door.

It was nearly an hour later when Ellen was able to wrest herself free of charts and checking on patients. As she turned the corner onto Mr. Rosen's hall, she came to an abrupt stop, her heart leaping up into her throat.

Three nurses stood against the wall outside Elliott's door, smiles playing across their rapt faces. Next to them several orderlies and residents had collected.

But what caused her cheeks to flame was the music of a full-blown symphony orchestra which was pouring out of Elliott Rosen's door.

Ellen nudged her way through the group at the door and hurried into the room. "What's going on here?" she demanded, her words coming out loud and quick. And then she stopped and looked around the cramped hospital room in amazement.

Sitting in the corner in Bermuda shorts and Topsiders was a bearded young man with a violin on his shoulder. Armand stood at the end of the bed holding a thermometer in his fingers like a baton. Lying on the bed beside Elliott's thin hip was a blaring tape recorder.

Ellen recognized the bearded man as the symphony's first violinist about the same time that her index finger jammed mercilessly into the Off button on the tape player. "What do you think you're doing?"

"Would you believe a rehearsal?" Elliott Rosen offered with a wonderful twinkle in his eye.

"No, I would not!" Ellen's eyes locked into Armand's. "Armand Dante, this is crazy, against the hospital rules, and just may cost me my job! The whole floor is awake!"

"And will fall asleep with mighty sweet dreams, Ellie. You can be sure of that."

Again it was Elliott who spoke; he seemed to be the only one who was willing to talk to her. His thin, tired body was full of life.

"Sorry, Ellen." Armand tried to look sheepish but failed miserably, his dark eyes sparkling with pleasure. "I knew George here was free after the concert, and when Elliott and I got to talking about the first movement of the Tchaikovsky Violin Concerto in D, well—"

"You thought you might as well have the real thing. Of course! I mean, doesn't everyone bring live music into a hospital room in the dead of night?" She put both fists firmly on her hips.

Armand sidled up to her and traced lazy patterns on the back of her starched uniform. "Well, now, why not? If you can have the real thing, why settle for less? George is brilliant in this piece! Perhaps you'd like to hear—"

"No!" Ellen threw her hands up in the air, trying at the same time to ignore the heated trails his fingers were leaving on her back. She nodded at George. "No offense, please, but I'd much rather catch you at the music hall. The acoustics, you understand." She finally managed a smile. No supervisors had shown up yet, and Elliott Rosen *did* look at least ten years younger. The color in his cheeks was brighter and healthier-looking than any medicine could have made it. And beneath her anxiety about disobeying hospital rules was the stirring knowledge that Armand Dante was a very kind, thoughtful man . . . a truly lovable man!

"Speaking of real things and wonderful music," Armand whispered into her ear, "how'd you like to meet me in the supply closet?"

"Armand, hush." Ellen's cheeks were blazing now, a close second to Mr. Rosen's. "George, thank you for coming, but at the risk of incurring Mr. Rosen's wrath, I'm going to kick you and Armand out."

Armand feigned a pained expression. "Dismissed without an encore! Do you think we can bear it, George?"

The young, good-looking violinist rose from the uncomfortable hospital chair and shook his head, laughing. "Well, it'll make an interesting story when the fellas are talking about how they spent Saturday evening." He smiled at the beaming man lying in the bed and bowed slightly. "Good night, Mr. Rosen. It's been a pleasure."

Elliott nodded back at the two men, a wonderful smile on his face.

Armand trailed after George as he walked down the hallway, catching Ellen's hand and pulling her into the shadows behind the nurses' station. "Angry with me?"

Ellen looked into the magical depths of his eyes and melted. How much longer would he cause this storm of emotion in her? she wondered. Surely her heartbeat would soon return to normal and she would be able to look at her relationship with

Armand in a calm, realistic way, with the coolness and levelheadedness Ellen Farrell was known for. Soon, surely . . . she thought as she closed her eyes and kissed her maestro full on the mouth.

The infamous evening of music, fun, and laughter in Elliott Rosen's hospital room caused rumors to race through the hospital.

Ellen heard her name drifting out of nurses' stations, elevators, and from the crowded tables in the staff cafeteria. But there was no time to dwell on it, to be bothered or pleased by it, or to try to correct the many incorrect assumptions, because two nights later her dearest friend in all the world calmly walked into the hospital shortly after midnight and gave birth to a beautiful, dark-haired, eight-pound baby girl.

Rick Westin was beside himself with joy as he hugged Ellen off her feet. "We did it, Ellen! We did it! Isn't she the most gorgeous baby you've ever seen?"

Ellen brushed tears from her eyes and pressed her face against the window separating them from tiny Kathleen Ellen Mary Westin. She was beautiful. Tiny and perfect and beautiful. Her very own goddaughter. Her namesake! A huge lump grew in her throat as she watched the baby sleep.

"Well, this explains everything. Congratulations, Rick." There was no mistaking the deep voice behind them. Ellen turned to face Armand and a huge furry black and white panda bear that was ten times bigger than the sleeping baby in the hospital bassinet.

"Oh, Armand—"

"Next time there's a celebration going on up here, I want to know about it!"

"I promise, darling." Ellen slipped an arm around his waist and leaned against him, tired and happy. She and Rick had been at the hospital all night, coaching Laurie with her breathing. There had been no time to call, no time for anything other than keeping pace with the glorious miracle taking place in their midst.

"How did you guess where to find us?" she asked, looking up into his beloved face.

"How do you suppose, my beauty?"

Ellen laughed wearily as they both nodded and muttered, "Clarence" in unison. Dear Clarence, who kept nearly as close track of Ellen as her mother had done for eighteen years. He would have told Armand that she'd never returned from yesterday's shift at the hospital.

Hugging her, Armand turned his attention back to the tiny baby in the bassinet, its perfect little hands curled in sleep. "What a little jewel," he said softly. "Congratulations again, Papa."

"Thanks, Armand! She is something, isn't she? And now I'm going to see my other best girl."

"Well, don't go empty-handed; here, I brought a few things to celebrate." Handing Rick the huge bear, he drew a bottle of champagne out of a sack he had propped against the wall. The champagne was followed by a box of the finest cigars and a bottle of Joy perfume. "For Laurie," he explained as Ellen hugged the breath out of him. Rick collected the gifts, threw his baby a kiss, and headed for Laurie's room.

"And for you, my sweet"—Armand gazed lovingly into her eyes—"I have a message from Clarence.

Your parents and sundry siblings are coming in at Laurie's family's suggestion—for the baby's baptism."

Ellen's mouth flew open and Armand gently tapped it closed.

"They'll stay a few days, Clarence says, to see a sight or two, then head back to Pennsylvania."

"Oh, Armand."

"Oh, Ellen," Armand echoed teasingly, then sealed this newest twist of fate with a kiss.

Helen and John Farrell were the salt of the earth—warm, loving, plain folks who rarely wandered much beyond the outskirts of Pittsburgh except to visit the central Pennsylvania farms where they had grown up. They were totally unprepared, as Ellen knew they would be, for what greeted them in Washington, D.C.

"Oh, my, honey, a . . . a hearse?" Helen hugged her oldest daughter as she looked apprehensively at the long, sleek black car parked at the airport curb.

John Farrell, a large, broad-shouldered man with a twinkle in his clear blue eyes, swept Ellen away from her mother and kissed her warmly, then stepped back and looked at the car. "It's not a hearse, Helen. It's a limo, right El?" He winked broadly.

"That's right, Daddy. It's . . . it—it belongs to a friend of mine who loaned it to us to use so you wouldn't have to rent a car while you're here."

"Awesome!" Freddie Farrell exclaimed from his perch on top of the pile of suitcases. At eleven years of age, Freddie spoke only when there was something worthwhile to speak about. Like limos. Cheryl and Karen, the fifteen-year-old twins, frowned sophisticatedly at Freddie's outburst as they stole glances at the shiny car.

"But, dear," Helen persisted, "do we really need a limo just to get from here to your apartment?"

She knew she should have warned them over the phone. But the past two weeks had rushed by so quickly: She and Armand had spent every free moment visiting at the hospital, and then Laurie and the baby had gone home, and Ellen had wanted to spend all the time she could holding the sweet-smelling infant who had already captured all their hearts and convinced Ellen perhaps she'd have six or so. Still, she knew now she should have said *something* sooner.

She mustered up all her courage and smiled brightly. "Guess what, Mom and Dad, I have a surprise for you and Freddie and the twins."

"A surprise, dear?" Mrs. Farrell looked confused.

"Well, my apartment is a little cramped, and I wasn't sure how many of the kids were coming with you, so this friend . . . you know—" she nodded at the car and went on quickly—"well, he . . . his symphony . . . keeps a suite at the Hilton for guest artists, and since it's not being used right now, he thought maybe you'd like to stay in it." There. It was all out.

"Symphony?"

"Suite!"

"Friend?"

"Ellen!"

The words all collided in the air, but it was her father's "Ellen!" that caused the chauffeur to roll the window down and ask if everything was all right.

"Yes, yes, Ernest, just fine, thank you," she mumbled, then faced her father quickly. "Dad, it makes perfect sense. The kids would have to sleep on the floor at my apartment and we'd be crawling all over one another. Even Laurie and I had trouble staying out of each other's way when we lived there together. This will work out fine, and be an even nicer vacation for all of you." She hugged her mother warmly. "Honest it will. Trust me." She chuckled to herself as she spoke Armand's oft repeated dictum. *Trust me.* And she did trust him. With her whole heart and soul.

"All right, Ellen Mary Farrell, I want to know about this friend." Her father's voice was kind but no-nonsense as they drove across the Potomac and toward the Hilton.

Helen Farrell listened to her husband and wondered whether he'd ever realize that his grown children were lovely, mature adults. Ellen certainly was, with a glow about her that made it difficult for Helen to tear her eyes away. And she could tell from the tilt of Ellen's head that she was wondering the same thing about her father. But Ellen loved and respected him far too much to ever say anything; she'd simply play along—and love him all the more for caring about her.

"His name is Armand Dante, Dad. He's a wonderful man. I know you'll all like him a lot." She glanced over at her mother for encouragement, and got more of a response than she'd expected.

"Armand Dante!" Helen sat up straight as an arrow. "Ellen, Armand Dante is someone—"

"Right!" John Farrell's thick graying brows drew together. "Yes, I've heard that name too."

Karen, Cheryl, and Freddie stopped their chatter to listen to Ellen's nervous reply.

"Well, yes, you may have. He's a conductor here—"

"On a train?" Freddie asked.

"No, silly. A symphony conductor. A musician, and a very fine one too."

"Oh." Freddie sank back into the seat, disappointed.

"Of course! He's been on television," Cheryl put in enthusiastically.

Helen looked over at her daughter. So *that* was the reason for Ellen's sudden glow. Now it all made sense: Her oldest daughter was in love. She touched her cheek absently. "A symphony conductor, Ellen?"

Ellen laughed. "I know what you're thinking, Mom. What's a man like Armand Dante doing with someone who flunked ninth grade choir?"

Her mother smiled gently. "Not at all, dear. You'd make any man a lovely . . . friend. But Armand Dante—he's, well, famous. A public figure."

"Oh, I'm well aware of that! And that's been hard at times, I'll admit. But I like him very, very much, Mom. And that makes it worth the other irritating stuff, like having my name pop up in a gossip column now and then, or—"

"What!" The twins were all ears now.

"Well, he's a well-known bachelor, and this silly column tends to record his movements like clockwork."

Frowning with discomfort, Ellen slid her gaze

away from her parents' startled faces. "Oh, look"—
she pointed out the window—"we're almost there!"

The limo slowed to a stop. The lavish hotel rose
before them, and Ellen breathed a sigh of relief. It
was difficult to talk about Armand. He wasn't the
kind of man one explained in a word or two. Perhaps not even in a lifetime.

The suite took their breath away, from the endless sweep of windows that looked out over the his-
toric city, to the crystal chandelier in the formal
dining room and the large-screen TV in the living
room, to the marble whirlpool bath surrounded by
mirrors and lush plants.

Helen Farrell sank down on a velvet couch and
sighed deeply. "Ellen, dear, how will we ever repay
your friend for all this?" She looked around at the
lovely basket of fruit on a glass-topped table, and
the champagne chilling in a silver bucket nearby.
A collection of tickets to the symphony, Rick
Westin's banjo show, and two plays were laid out
next to a stack of current videocassettes for the television, should they need a quiet time. The bar and
refrigerator were stocked, directions to the indoor
and outdoor pool printed out, and fresh flowers
overflowed from crystal vases. Nothing was left
undone.

Ellen realized with a start that the thought of
repaying Armand had never entered her mind.
There was no need even to consider such a thing.
He didn't expect it or want it. Armand was doing all
of this because—yes, she thought, a smile lighting
her face—because he loved her. "Repay him? Don't
worry about it, Mom. He's not that way."

Her father looked at her skeptically. "Well then,

what way is he? Just when do we get to meet this wonderful person?"

"Tomorrow. He's all tied up in rehearsals today, but he'll be at the christening in the morning. He loves little Kathleen nearly as much as I do. And the brunch will be at his house since he has the most room. Rick and Laurie's place is small and mine's even smaller, so he offered—"

She realized she was chatting like a magpie, but couldn't seem to stop herself. She tossed her head. "Tomorrow! You'll all meet tomorrow. Now, anyone for a swim?"

Ellen smoothed her new coral-colored silk dress nervously and straightened her wide-brimmed hat. A bundle of emotions as varied as the people in the church threatened to overwhelm her, but she refused to allow it. Not today. Such a hodgepodge of different people, she thought with a sudden smile. Laurie and Rick, her plain and simple parents, and Armand, who couldn't look or act simple if he devoted twenty lifetimes to it. All the people who made up the fabric of her life.

Laurie stepped up beside her and placed the sleeping baby in her arms. Ellen smiled at Laurie, then looked down at the infant, and all other thoughts drifted away as she watched the tiny mouth moving in sleep, the butterfly fringe of lashes lying on her soft, plump cheeks. Proudly Ellen took her place next to the priest at the baptismal font.

From a distance, standing off to the side beside a pillar in the old stone church, Armand Dante was watching. All was a blur except for the lovely woman in the shining silk dress who had somehow slipped into his life and stolen his heart. He wasn't even sure how it had happened, or why. It simply had. And he knew his life would never be the same.

He had introduced himself to her parents on the church steps and knew they were watching him now from their places in the church pews, wondering who in heaven's name this man was who had taken over their oldest daughter's life. John Farrell was very protective of his children, whatever their ages; Armand could tell that in a glance. He suddenly wanted to assure the older man that there was nothing in this world he would ever do to hurt Ellen, nothing he'd deny her, if only she'd share his life. Because without her he had no life.

Helen and John Farrell knelt in the first pew beside three of their six children, watching the small group gather around the lovely old marble font. Memories of baptisms from years gone by flashed before Helen's eyes in vivid detail. And now her own Ellen, a lovely grown woman, stood there with a baby in her arms. Her eyes shifted to the man whose eyes hadn't left Ellen since they'd all taken their places in the church, the darkly handsome man in the expensive, tailored suit, the man who seemed bigger than life to Helen and John. He loved Ellen, there was no question in Helen's mind about that. But Armand Dante's life had a magnitude about it that seemed too harsh a contrast to the simple values upon which her own family's life was built. And that was frightening to both her and her husband, because they knew their daughter's happiness was at stake.

The baby's awakening cry drew everyone's attention back to the front of the small vestibule, and Ellen cradled the infant gently, soothing away her fears. With a clear voice she accepted responsibility as tiny Kathleen's godmother, repeating the age-old prayers after the priest. And when the ceremony was over, Ellen smiled and did nothing to stop the flow of tears that collected in the corners of her eyes and streamed down her cheeks.

Everyone agreed that Armand's home was the perfect place for Kathleen Ellen's first brunch.

The wonderful two-story apartment boasted more square footage than the farm where he was born, John Farrell thought with amusement.

The great room was two stories high and was filled with white sunlight pouring though ten-foot-tall windows. The grand piano was filled now with a pile of colorfully wrapped baby gifts that grew continuously as guests arrived. Soft classical music provided a wonderful background for the happy chatter of the crowd.

"Armand, everything is perfect," Laurie whispered as she kissed him gently on the cheek.

"Ah, my little mother, so I've finally won you over?"

Laurie looked momentarily surprised. "What do you mean?"

Armand smiled gently. "Please, I don't mean to make you uncomfortable, Laurie. I meant only that you have been very 'cautious,' shall we say, about my relationship with Ellen."

Laurie was still for just a moment, then she met his dark gaze sincerely. "Yes, Armand, I was. I still am . . . a little. Because you're still you: a wonderful, loving man, but from a whole different world than Ellen and I are accustomed to." She fingered the lacy ruffle on her dress as her eyelids dropped for a moment in thought, and then she faced him again. "But I do know that your feelings for Ellen are sincere. I wasn't so sure of that in the beginning, but I know now that Ellen can trust you."

"You just don't know if she can live my kind of life, is that it?" he questioned softly.

"Or you, hers, Armand. You're very different people."

Armand looked at Ellen's closest friend for a long moment, knowing that what she'd said was absolutely true. But just as certain, Armand felt with the deepest conviction, was the fact that those differences could never matter in any great way. He would never hurt Ellen. She could trust him with her life.

"There you two are." Ellen burst breathlessly into the kitchen, where they were talking. "Kathleen is feeling slighted, Laurie; everyone is eating but her. And you, Armand"—she linked her arm comfortably in his and grinned up into his ebony eyes—"you are in demand. Everyone is eager to meet their wonderful host."

Ellen drew him back into the large room and into the swarm of people waiting to meet Armand Dante.

She watched her father and could almost read his mind. At first he stood silently near the piano, watching Armand carefully, his square face expressionless. Then, with a determined look in his eyes, he approached Armand, and Ellen could see that her lover was in for an interview to rival that of any reporter he'd ever dealt with. She rushed off into the safety of the kitchen to check on the food.

Armand smiled as Ellen's father approached him, and the two shook hands cordially.

"So, Armand, you are a good friend of Ellen's?" John Farrell's gruffness was friendly, and Armand met his direct look easily. It was as clear and honest as Ellen's.

"Yes, sir, we've become quite close. I think Ellen is the finest woman I've ever met."

Ellen's father nodded. "That she is. A fine, simple gal. Of all my kids, Ellen's the easiest to read. What she wants from life is as direct and plain as the nose on your face." He paused for Armand to comment, but he held his silence and John went on. "Yep. Being a nurse, helping people. Having lots of kids. El's terrific with kids, always was. Used to baby-sit all the kids in the neighborhood and loved every minute of it."

Armand smiled. "There isn't much Ellen isn't good at. She's very special."

"Yes."

"I love your daughter, Mr. Farrell."

"Yes. I thought as much, from the look on your face when you watched her. And," he said, sighing, "if I'm not way off base, I do believe my daughter loves you as well."

"I certainly hope so." Armand held himself still, but his heart was racing. This was tougher than any musical performance he'd ever given. "Mr. Farrell—" he began, but the other man cut him short.

"Better make that *John*. Looks like we're going to get to know each other pretty well."

"Thank you, John."

"You're welcome, Armand. *Armand!*"John Farrell shook his head. "Darned if I ever expected that."

"Your daughter had a little trouble with it at first also." Armand laughed, a rich, honest sound that made the older man smile.

"Well, if she got past that hurdle, maybe the rest will be easy."

"I'll try to make it as easy as possible, John. I love her a great deal!"

Later, after the ride back to the hotel, John Farrell beckoned his daughter aside. "Feel like taking a little walk to stretch our legs, El?"

"Love to, Dad," she said, looping her arm through his.

They walked slowly around the block, comfortable in each other's silence. Then Ellen said softly, "Well? What do you think, Dad?"

"No beating around the bush, Ellen dear?"

"No."

"All right then. I think he is talented, intelligent, compassionate. A fine man, El . . . perhaps a wonderful man. But I think there are many differences between the two of you, your experiences, your expectations. His life must be as difficult as it is exciting. Could you live that kind of life?"

"I don't know, Dad," she whispered, unable to be anything but honest. "I think so! I want to, because I really love him. Very, very much." She slipped an arm around her father's waist and leaned her cheek on his shoulder. "Daddy, do you think I could do it? Dare I try?"

Her father hugged her close, this grown-up

daughter of his who was still his little girl. "Ah, I wish I had some simple answer. But only you can know that. Your heart alone holds the answer to that question."

Eight

"I'm going to steal you away for the weekend, Armand! We'll have two days, nearly three, together!" Ellen clutched the phone excitedly, her blue eyes flashing with anticipation.

"I'm yours, my love!" With the thought came a surge of arousal so strong, it made even his teeth ache. "Listen, I've the perfect plan—"

"Armand—"

"No, listen to me. I have no performances, and you need a rest from the frantic activity of the past weeks: work, the baby, your family. I know the perfect way to slow your metabolism back to normal."

"Armand, the day you slow down my metabolism will be a cold day in—"

"Ellen!" Armand teased. "Such talk from an almost nun! Now, listen to me for a moment, my love. The forecast is for a few days of Indian summer: sunny skies, warm days, and nights . . . ah, idyllic nights! We'll take the yacht down the Bay and out into the ocean."

His husky voice raced on. "I'll have Thomas and the crew get it ready immediately. They'll have to stock the kitchen, order flowers, freshen the beds, of course, but it shouldn't take long. It will be wonderful!"

"The crew?" Ellen felt lost for a moment, her voice a whisper in the emptiness of her apartment.

"Yes, the captain and five sailors. Henri has two to help him in the kitchen. But it's as if we're all alone on the ship. And it's wonderful on the ocean at this time of year. The moon is unbelievable, and the sky at high noon is the color of your eyes."

"Armand, no!"

"Why not? What's the matter, Ellen?" A sharp stab of disappointment gave way to concern. "Seasickness, is that it? We can take care of—"

"No, Armand, I don't get seasick."

"Good. Then we'll leave in four hours?"

"No, Armand, wait. Please listen to me." Ellen frowned. The roller coaster was taking off again, but she was determined to stop it, or at least slow it down. "Armand, you've been so wonderful these past weeks, making all those . . . those absolutely perfect plans for my family, for Laurie and Rick and the baby. And most of all, for me. You've wined me and dined me, entertained me, and swept me into your incredible world with the force of a tornado!"

Armand gave a deep, pleased laugh. "That's just what I wanted to do!"

"I know. But now it's my turn. I want to please you!"

"But you do, my love, each moment I'm with you!"

Her heart took a little leap of joy. How had she ever gotten so lucky? "Thank you, Armand. But wait just a moment. I called you, remember, so I get to talk. Now, I want to plan these two days—down to the very smallest detail. I'm going to take you out to the beach and show you how I have fun. I want to share my world with you, the things I like to do, the places I love." She paused, then added lightly, "Believe it or not, I don't usually round up the crew and sail off into an ocean sunset."

"But it's so beautiful, Ellen. You would love it."

Damn, he was being difficult. Of course she'd love it . . . sailing off like that, not only in the lap of luxury, but in Armand's lap to boot! But not this time. No, it was important that she do it her way this time.

"I'm sure I would," she finally managed to state matter-of-factly, "but not this time. This is my weekend, Armand, and I want to plan every second of it for you. I want to sweep you off your feet."

"You've already done that, Ellen," he said softly.

Ellen chose her next words carefully. "Maybe we've done that to each other. But I'm serious about this. I think your yacht sounds romantic and wonderful, but it's time you saw me in my own world, learned about the things I do when I need to air out the cobwebs and let my hair down. It's time, Maestro, that you learned how the other half lives."

Armand held his silence as echoes of Laurie's and John Farrell's concerns drifted through his thoughts. Oh, he knew exactly what Ellen was doing. She was testing the waters, seeing if he could, in fact, fit into her world.

Armand shook his dark head and smiled to himself as love for Ellen filled his soul. He'd fit into a peanut shell for this woman if it would make her happy. Aloud, his rich voice was filled with laughter. "Plan away, my beauty, and I'll be there with bells on. Or off, if you so desire. Your wish is my command."

It was barely two hours later when Ellen pulled into a parking spot just down the block from Armand's elegant building. Her car was crammed from floor to ceiling with things she'd packed for the trip, and she snapped down the locks to protect her treasures and then hurried to fetch the best treasure of them all, that gorgeous hunk of a conductor she was kidnapping for the weekend!

She smiled to herself in sheer pleasure. This was going to be wonderful! Romantic. Private. Just the two of them, the ocean, a quiet stretch of beach . . . *heaven!*

But where was that man? Narrowing her eyes against the sunlight, she caught a movement at the canopied doorway of his building, and her heart began to beat faster, just as it did each time she saw him.

But it wasn't Armand who hurried down the steps. Ellen stepped back quickly, just in time to avoid a head-on collision with an expensively dressed woman. Her finely shaped brows were knit into a tight line that matched that of her lips; her eyes were flashing with anger.

Ellen stared curiously as the woman slipped her enviable figure into the bright yellow sports car at the curb, ground the gears to life, and sped off down the street without a backward glance.

Ellen's eyes shifted back to the door.

Armand stood quietly on the top step, his hands clenched into tight fists. He was staring after the car.

"Armand . . ."

His eyes jerked toward her. "Ellen! Love!" He rushed down the steps to her side and wrapped her in his arms.

Ellen felt the tension drain from his muscles. She looked up into the flashing darkness of his eyes. "Wow, even the sidewalks are getting dangerous!" Her voice was light and teasing. "Who was that, Armand? A friend of yours? She didn't seem very happy."

"No, she's not a friend of mine. Just someone I used to know, looking to settle an old score." Armand's voice was tight and controlled, giving few clues.

"Oh?" Ellen waited patiently for an explanation of his cryptic remark, but none followed. "Well, who won?"

"No one," he answered softly, smiling down into her wide blue eyes. "I told her the game was called—on account of love."

He kissed her lightly, a gossamer touch of tenderness. Then he flashed that heart-stopping grin of his. "Okay, I'm yours. Do with me as you will!"

The man was irresistible.

Matching his grin, Ellen led Armand to the car, hopped into the driver's seat, and beckoned him inside.

He took one glance at the poles and stakes and waterproof nylon sheeting stuffed into the back seat, the rolled-up sleeping bag, and the bags and baskets of provisions. "You're sure there's room for me?" he asked with a laugh.

"If not, I'll leave everything lying here in the middle of the street. You, sir, are all I want!"

"No need to get melodramatic," he teased, but his dark face was flushed with pleasure. Without another word he good-naturedly wedged himself in between a straw basket filled with bread and the car door.

"Ready?" Ellen beamed and pulled away from the curb.

Armand turned and looked at her, his eyes moving slowly from her face down to her tennis shoes and back up again. Her hair was tied back with a bright blue ribbon and she was dressed in faded blue jeans and a plaid shirt with the sleeves rolled up.

"Ellen, you are the most beautiful woman I've ever seen," he said finally, his voice low and husky.

Ellen laughed nervously, blushing beneath the intensity of his gaze. "Thank you, kind sir," she managed, welcoming the cool breeze that blew through the open windows as she headed the car north.

They grew silent then, each lost in the pleasure of the other's nearness.

"Where are we going?" Armand asked finally as Ellen left the busy city behind.

Ellen threw him a mischievous grin. "Trust me."

"Oh, I do. With my life," Armand retorted with a husky laugh. "But I'd feel much better if I knew where that life was headed."

"North, then northeast."

"Which should put us quite neatly into the middle of the Bay," he said laughingly.

"Wrong, Maestro. We're headed across the bridge at Annapolis, then over to the ocean. It's a trip I've made many times since I started working in Washington."

Ellen's voice was softened by memories, and Armand edged closer to listen, the bread basket now balanced awkwardly on his knees.

"I've gone alone before," she said with a shy smile. "It's a place my family visited several times when I was a child, and I kind of rediscovered it when I moved back here. I love it. It's lovely and fresh and uncomplicated. And the ocean's magic always slows life down for me and puts everything back in its right and proper place."

Armand was quiet. A curious realization dawned on him at that instant: He had swept Ellen up in such a fast, passionate romance that she hadn't had time to share much of her private world with him. He might have missed this special moment. As the car sped across the flat coastal plain of the Eastern shore, past horsedrawn Amish buggies that were nearly as numerous as resort-bound cars, through lush farmland and pungent-smelling woods, he vowed silently never to make that mistake again.

"We're here at last." Ellen pulled the car into the small public parking lot and stretched her arms as far above her head as the small car would allow.

"Where?" Armand raised himself from the cramped position he had folded himself into hours before and peered curiously through the windshield. Endless darkness stretched out before them. Warily he asked, "This is it?"

Ellen tossed him a happy grin. "What you see is what you get."

"But, *cara*"—one dark brow rose in amusement—"I don't see *anything*."

"Then listen!"

The roar of the ocean filled the night air.

Armand opened the door and let his cramped body fall out onto the sandy lot.

Ellen scooted over on the seat and fished a flashlight out of the glove compartment. "Here," she tossed it out after Armand. "Look around. And if this isn't the grandest hotel room you've ever been lured into, I don't want to hear about it."

"Certainly the largest," Armand murmured as the impact of her words slowly began to register in his sleepy mind. "We—you and I—are going to sleep here?"

Ellen was beside him now, one arm wrapped around his waist as she inhaled the tangy sea air. "Yes, my dear Maestro. You and I, with heaven hanging above us."

A few blinking stars lit the shore as their eyes adjusted to the night, and they walked arm in arm along the sandy beach.

"Well? What do you think?" Ellen asked at last.

"I think, my love, it is a marvelous hotel, a marvelous beach. And you"—he pulled her against him and nibbled on her lower lip, his hands sliding eagerly inside her flannel shirt—"you are the most marvelous thing of all! Come back here!" he demanded as she slipped from his arms, laughing softly deep in her throat.

"Oh, no! We have to set up camp first!"

"What? Come here. I want to love you."

"Work before pleasure!" And with little puffs of sand kicking up from her sneakers, she raced him down the beach.

They found a tiny cove sheltered by the dunes and there, with a single flashlight and the stars above to light their efforts, Armand helped Ellen pitch the small nylon tent. As he rummaged around inside, trying to convince himself this truly was a wonderful idea, Ellen busied herself sorting through the sacks of groceries she'd hauled down from the car.

"Armand?" she called through the tiny tent window. "Come out here for a moment. I have a surprise for you."

"I think I've had enough surprises for one day," he grumbled loudly. But curiosity got the better of him, and in moments he poked his head out the tiny tent door.

Ellen was sitting beside a small fire she had made in the center of a ring of rocks. Beside her was a plateful of crackers and cheese, and next to that, chilling in the cool sand, was a bottle of champagne. "Here"—she motioned him down beside her and handed him a crystal champagne glass—"would you like a bedtime snack?"

Her eyes, sparkling in the firelight, wove a spell of enchantment around Armand. He sank into the soft sand and pulled her close against his eager body. "That is not the hunger that needs satisfying," he murmured against the pulse point at her temple. Then his lips moved slowly across her face, dusting kisses on her eyelids and cheeks. He stopped, his mouth just inches from hers, his breath warm on her lips as he whispered, "Ellen, I love you."

Lifting her face that last inch to his, she parted her lips to drink in the kiss he offered.

And then they made love beneath the stars, on into the night until the embers finally faded away and sleep pulled a dreamy blanket over the two still figures curled inside a single sleeping bag beside the empty tent.

"How did you sleep?" Ellen asked with a loving smile as she scrambled eggs in a black iron skillet. "You tossed and turned a bit and mumbled something that sounded like 'take this hand.' "

Armand stood, yawning and stretching his cramped muscles. When he looked at her, one dark brow swooped up. "It was probably 'take this *sand.*' Half of the beach was there *in* the sleeping bag with us, I'm quite sure."

Ellen's laughter echoed among the dunes. "*The Prince and the Pea,* is that it? *I* didn't feel any sand at all." She leaned over and set the skillet on the glowing coals. In minutes the smell of pork sausages and eggs filled the air. Handing a plateful to Armand, she slipped down beside him on the sand. "This sea air is like a drug for me. It makes me feel loose and free—and I sleep like a baby."

Armand stopped eating long enough to drop a gentle kiss on her shoulder. "And here I thought I was the one who did that to you."

"Oh," she said happily, "you too. Yes, Armand, you most definitely influence my sleeping habits."

"Good. That is one of my top priorities."

Armand watched her, thinking how lovely she

looked with the sunlight on her, the soft wind blushing her cheeks. "I'm happy here with you. Happier than I can remember being."

"It's the magic of this place," she told him, smiling.

"It's *your* magic, love." He stood and dusted the sand from his tan slacks, then offered her a hand up. "Now, what's in store for us the rest of this great day? Shall I find us a sailboat for charter? Or would you like to drive along the coast? Or"—he grinned at her lasciviously—"shall we, as the natives say, have a roll in the sand?"

Ellen's laughter curled around him as she slipped out of his embrace. "None of the above. You, Maestro, are going to help me catch our dinner." And she quickly doused the fire with sand, scooped up the dishes, and headed back toward the trunk of her car.

Armand was totally mystified by the assortment of things Ellen pulled from the trunk and lugged down to the beach: plastic buckets and small nets, an assortment of shovels, and several round boxes of salt. In minutes they were back down on the beach, and Armand was dutifully hauling sacks and following Ellen around a bend in the cove and on down the beach. Here the peninsula narrowed and fishermen, armed with poles and nets, lined the shore.

"Armand, you amaze me," Ellen threw back over one shoulder as she skirted a huge boulder jutting out into the water.

"Oh? Did you think I would melt when the water touched me?"

"No, no. Not that." She laughed. "It's your blind faith. You have no idea what's happening to you, yet you're following me as dutifully as a puppy. Such trust!"

"Of course, *cara*. Trust is the only way."

It was only light banter, words meant to fill the space between them, but suddenly Ellen's thoughts were pulled back to the woman rushing down Armand's steps the day before, and she bit her lip to silence the question that nearly escaped. No, she wouldn't impose on his privacy. She would trust him. She would.

"You're right!" Dropping her load of things on the shore, she linked one arm through his. "Now, do you see that fellow out there?" She pointed to a fisherman wading in the shallow water with a dip net in one hand and a plastic bucket in the other. "He has a head start on us, but if we dip in now, we'll have more crabs than we can eat by dinnertime."

And they did, enough for a steamed crab feast that completely satisfied appetites made ravenous by hours in the crisp fall air.

Later they spent the evening hours watching the crimson embers die away and weary fishermen shuffle off in the distance, their day's catch heavy behind them in huge weathered sacks. Armand lay on his side, his head in Ellen's lap, drawing hearts in the sand like a kid.

"A.D. loves E.F." He grinned. "And E.F. loves A.D., right?" He drew arrows through the hearts, chuckling softly against the warm sandy skin of her thighs. "I do love you, Ellen. And I'd like to tell the whole world!"

"I have a feeling the whole world knows every-thing already." Ellen sighed, the words slipping out before she could think about what she was saying.

Armand stiffened and turned to stare into her honest blue eyes. "That really bothers you, doesn't it?"

She shrugged, trying to make light of the whole thing. "A little, yes."

"But you do love me, don't you?"

"Of course I do!" *Love him?* The words didn't do justice to the emotion that filled her heart and soul. Of course she loved him—deeply, almost painfully. "I wouldn't be here with you tonight like this if I didn't love you."

"Then what do you fear?" Armand wrapped his arms around her and pulled her into the warmth of his embrace.

"It's not really fear—" she began, but stumbled over her words. She didn't know how to explain the worry that beat at her heart like a dark wing.

"What is it then, love? Tell me, what makes you hesitate?" He kissed her gently at the hollow of her neck, and Ellen's limbs melted like Jell-O. Here in his arms she felt safe, and her worries seemed foolish. Without answering, she pressed her cheek against his, loving the rough shadow of his beard.

They sat there, then, in silence, with only the stars and the murmuring sea for company. Finally Armand spoke. "Ellen, is it my life that frightens you?"

Ellen scooped up a handful of sand and let it filter slowly through her fingers. "In a small way, yes, I guess it is, Armand. This peaceful, simple time today, without reporters and fans and people who want your attention, it felt so good!"

"I know that. And I feel the same way." He

splayed his fingers beneath her breasts, kneading the smooth soft skin. "But there will always be days like today, escapes—"

"*Escapes* . . . maybe that's it, Armand. It frightens me that we have to find time to escape, to arrange privacy."

"No." He hushed her fear with his deep soothing voice. "*Everyone* has to do that now and again. Isn't that what you were doing the very day I met you? Escaping along the highway, looking for privacy, a chance to be alone with—"

"My screams?" She laughed huskily. "Yes, perhaps that's true, Armand." She had long since told him about Dan Newlin, and the reason she was driving along the highway at eighty miles per hour.

"Well then? And if this is what you like, if this is what makes you happy"—his broad hand swept the isolated beach—"then this is what we shall have as our private getaway. Now, if it's a *highway* you want," he whispered gently into her hair, tickling her ear, "that may take some doing!"

Ellen's laughter drifted off on the wind. "Oh, Armand, you're impossible. I can't think when you do that to me." She turned her head enough to bring her lips up to his and smother his answering laughter with a kiss.

Finally she pulled away and looked thoughtfully into the red glow of the dying fire. "Sometimes, Armand, I feel I know you better than I know my own soul, but at other times I'm not sure. There's a part of you, of your life, that's still alien and unknown to me. I think that's what frightens me."

Armand answered slowly, his fingers gently caressing her back. He knew it was important to Ellen that he handle her fear seriously, and honestly. She felt so fragile beneath his hand, like a tiny bird who needed someone to soothe it, give it strength to fly that last stretch to safety.

"Ellen, you know me better than anyone ever has. You know my fears, you've felt my love. The things you don't know about me—stories of my childhood, my family, the past—there'll be time to share all that. Maybe when we're both in rocking chairs, watching the surf come in, and we've had our fill of all there is to discover and love and cherish about each other, then we can divulge past secrets and laugh at our youthful foibles."

Spreading one leg on either side of her, Armand dug his bare feet into the damp sand and pulled her back against the hard wall of his chest. "What do you think, my beauty?" He nuzzled his head into the nape of her neck, tasting the salt and sweetness of her. "Does that make sense to you?"

Every inch of Ellen's body responded to his touch, her heart pounding in her chest, her blood racing beneath her heated skin. Every nerve ending was awakened to this strong, desiring man pressing her closer and closer until all thought of what did or didn't make sense was blocked out, all reason was smothered in the passion of their love.

Ellen's eyes were still closed as she reached out across the smooth sleeping bag, her fingers stretching for the comforting warmth of Armand beside her.

She sat up with a start, her eyes wide open. Late morning sunlight streamed in the tiny netted window and fell on the empty stretch of sleeping bag beside her. It was still hollowed from the weight of Armand's body.

"Armand?" Reaching for a T-shirt and jeans, Ellen quickly dressed and slipped through the flap of the tent. It must be almost noon, she realized, chagrined that she had slept so late. As she shielded her eyes from the sun, she scanned the beach for Armand's familiar long-legged form. But the beach was empty except for two old fishermen who had laid claim to a tiny stretch of shoreline a few hundred feet away.

Armand was nowhere in sight.

"Well, I guess I've turned him into a real beach-comber. He's probably out collecting breakfast," she mused aloud, her lips curving in a smile.

But the screech of brakes and the clatter of gravel from the parking lot up past the dunes told her otherwise.

Armand leaped from the car and hurried down the slope, calling to her as he ran.

"Armand, what's the matter? Where have you been?" Ellen's smile vanished.

"Nothing is the matter, love. Everything is great! Come, hurry."

Ellen stared after him as he turned and strode back toward the car. Finally, spurred by curiosity, she followed.

Armand gunned the engine as soon as Ellen slipped into the car, and then he peeled out of the parking lot. A folded piece of paper was wedged firmly between his fingers and the steering wheel.

"Armand, I haven't even washed my face! Where are we going?"

"A surprise, darling. Trust me."

In minutes the small car turned onto a narrow

gravel road and once again headed toward the water. Several large frame houses dotted the area as they neared the beach.

And there at the end of the beach was a rambling white house, bright blue shutters bordering the windows and a wide welcoming porch sweeping around all four sides of the two-story structure. A low, freshly painted picket fence defined the property line and was brightened by colorful patches of wildflowers.

Armand was out of the car before Ellen had registered that it was no longer moving. He waited at the gate, then ushered her through with a grand sweep.

"Armand, who lives here? Where are we going? Are these friends of yours?"

"Shhh, my love. Too many questions." He kissed her quickly before guiding her up the painted wooden steps and around to the front of the house.

The front faced the ocean, and the porch widened there to make room for groups of comfortable wicker chairs, wide porch swings, and huge pots of plants. Steps led down to a narrow wooden boardwalk that wound its way to the shore.

"What a beautiful spot, Armand," Ellen breathed, then added quickly, "but what are we doing here?" She touched his arm, a suspicion slowly taking root in her mind. "Oh, Armand, no . . . You didn't . . . *did you*?"

Her eyes were round as saucers as she faced him, her cheeks flushed. "No, Armand!"

He unfolded the realtor's paper he still held in his hand. "The real estate agent just showed it to me this morning. A getaway . . . privacy . . . just what you ordered! So what do you think? Say the word and it's yours. A perfect place to spend every weekend of the hundred years or so I plan on spending with you." His dark eyes sparkled. "And it has beds . . . *soft* beds, *sandless* beds."

"Oh, Armand." Ellen wrapped her arms around his neck, tears building up behind her lids. "It's lovely, but we . . . I—I don't need this. A simple tent . . ."

How did he do this to her so easily? she wondered. He turned her life into a whirlwind, turned the simplest whimsy into a dream of such incredible proportions that it took her breath away. Oh, he was wonderful, loving, kind . . . that was *why* he did it. But how could she, Ellen Farrell, R.N., handle it all?

"Armand Dante, you take my breath away. I don't know what to say."

Armand watched her carefully, trying to will away the confusion he saw building beneath her soft hesitant smile.

Damn! He was rushing again. He needed to slow down, not overwhelm her. Drawing a deep breath, he smiled and rubbed her cheek softly with one finger. "I'm doing it again, aren't I? I'm sorry. But I love you so much, I just want to make you happy; I want to give you everything! For the first time in my life, I feel—"

He paused, swallowed, his eyes darkening with emotion. He looked suddenly vulnerable and boyish. "Ellen, for the first time I feel I can give someone a part of myself. Not just my music. Remember, I told you my parents sent me away from home when I was eleven? Certainly they wanted the best for me. But—but they, and my teachers, my mentors, everyone seemed in awe of my talent. They gave me everything: time and instruction, encouragement, but all they would let me give back was the music. They held me at arm's length. But you! You let me into your heart. You love me for all that I am, I know it! For my hopes and fears and dreams—"

"And grand gestures!"

"Yes, even my grand gestures." He laughed softly, rubbing his cheek against her hair. "I do tend to make those, don't I? But Ellen, don't condemn me for that. I love you. And I love the things you love. Even tents are nice! And sand isn't so bad. . . ." He kissed her tenderly and slipped the piece of paper into the back pocket of her jeans. "We'll make it work, Ellen. Don't worry; there's nothing to be afraid of. Just trust me."

Nine

"Sometimes everything goes right, you know, Laurie?" Ellen's happy laughter echoed over the phone line. "I mean, it was perfect. Everything's perfect!"

"You mean you've stopped looking for lucky pennies on the sidewalk and crossing your fingers and wishing on first stars, kiddo?"

"Yup! Well, almost stopped," she admitted with a soft little chuckle. "But really, you wouldn't have believed Armand. There was sand in his sleeping bag, sand in his coffee—sand in his shorts!—and he loved it. He didn't even have to say so. I could see it in his eyes. He was relaxed and happy. He loved every minute of it!"

Laurie gave an almost inaudible sigh. "Well, you're right. I *wouldn't* have believed it. But if you say so—"

"I *do* say so!" Ellen snapped, suddenly angry. Her brows were a dark line above her clouded eyes.

"Why do you keep doing that to me, Laurie? I just spoke to my parents and they at least sounded pleased. If they can trust my feelings, why can't you? You're supposed to be my best friend!"

"I am your best friend. That's why I worry about you."

"Well, stop worrying and be happy for me!"

"Ellen, I can worry and be happy at the same time. It's one of those secret things they teach you in the convent!"

They both laughed, the tension between them dissolving. Laurie picked up the thread of the conversation. "So, I'm glad you had a terrific time. Both of you."

"That's better, Mrs. Westin. When are you going to realize how lucky I am?"

"When he realizes how lucky he is and proves it by walking down the aisle with you."

"Laurie! Armand doesn't have to prove anything. He loves me."

"Understandable! When you're not such a grump, you're extremely lovable. Now I'm going to feed the baby. It's almost ten and she's got an appetite like her godmother!"

"Good girl! Give her a hug for me, and I'll call when I get home from work in the morning. If I'm lucky, Rick'll answer. 'Bye!" Ellen hung up the phone with a smile on her face.

Fifteen minutes later she was dressed in her nurses' whites and pulling into the employee parking lot behind the hospital. The night was cool and clear and a golden slipper of a moon hung in the dark sky. Ellen pulled her jacket closer around her and hopped out of the car. She had just enough time to make a dash past the corner playground to

Tony's, a little Italian deli a block away that made the most incredible pepperoni pizza. One slice and she could face the trials and tribulations of the graveyard shift. And she'd get Mr. Rosen a package of those raisin cookies he loved because they reminded him of the ones his mother used to bake.

Late as it was, there was a pick-up game going on amid yells and cheers on the playground's basketball court, and there were people out on the streets. She smiled at them all: the two boys playing bebop music on the corner with a harmonica, a trash-can cover, and a set of drumsticks; an old couple walking arm in arm; three girls sitting on the fender of an old Chevy gossiping and laughing in the dark.

It was a perfectly beautiful evening, and she was smiling as she followed the spicy aroma of pizza into Tony's deli.

"Hi, gorgeous!" Tony winked at her over the counter, sending a pale disk of dough whirling into the air. "How's things?"

"Fantastic!" she exclaimed, winking back and remembering how his greeting used to make her feel strangely shy. Not anymore! Now she *felt* gorgeous. "Got a slice of pepperoni for me?"

"Does Dolly Parton have . . . wigs?" he tossed back with a grin. "Here ya go, fresh from Tony's oven!" He slid a hot spicy wedge across the counter on a sheet of waxed paper.

"Ummm . . . thanks," Ellen answered around her first bite. She reached into her pocketbook for money to pay for the pizza and cookies, and her little compact of blush slipped to the floor, its mirrored interior splintering into a dozen pieces.

"Oh, no!" she yelped.

"Whoa, seven years bad luck." Tony laughed, sending the delivery boy to fetch the broom. Then he saw Ellen's wide eyes and furrowed brow. "Hey, it's okay. The kid'll get it, no problem." He narrowed his eyes. "You don't believe those old superstitions, now, do ya?"

"Of course not!" Ellen lied, crossing the fingers of one hand behind her back. "Listen, I'm really sorry—"

"Like I said, no problem. And the food's on the house. Stop worryin', gorgeous."

"Who's worried?" she teased back, tossing her hair. And she wasn't, she realized with surprise. Who could worry when everything was perfect?

Ellen strolled back up the street, munching her pizza, timing her last bite to coincide with her arrival at the emergency room door.

"Hi, gang," she called to the cluster of nurses and residents gathered around the charting desk.

"Hey, it's our own Miss Virginia Symphony!" one of the doctors joked, enjoying his own humor.

"Funny, Henry, funny," Ellen said, hiding her annoyance behind a smile.

"Ellen, did you really spend the weekend on his yacht? That's what it said in Saturday's gossip column!" Adeline hurried around to the front of the desk and linked her arm through Ellen's with conspiratorial glee. "Ooooh, I want to hear all about it! Let's ditch these peasants and—"

"Watch who you two are calling peasants!"

"*I'm* not calling anyone peasants!" Ellen dug her heels in and shrugged off Adeline's grip. "Please, can we cut this out? I've told you all before, it makes me really uncomfortable when you all joke this way." Her usually clear eyes were clouded with concern.

"Who's joking?" came the sharp retort, arousing a spatter of cold stinging laughter.

Ellen frowned, fighting the heat that had risen to her face. "You had all better be! It just so happens Armand and I spent the weekend camping. Crabbing up on the Bay. Just—"

"Just like regular folks!" Henry quipped, but he slung an arm over her shoulder in a phony hug when Ellen glared at him. "Joke! Just a joke! Where's your sense of humor, Farrell?"

"Probably the same place your hair has gone to, Henry," she said, patting his bald spot and eliciting a titter of laughter from the group.

"Touché."

But she didn't feel as though she had won. Or even scored a point. She felt strangely deflated, and when she hung her jacket in her locker, she felt goose bumps rise on her arms. She just wanted to work her shift and hurry home in the morning to the warmth and security of Armand's arms.

It was a quiet shift: a mild case of food poisoning, a dog bite, a dislocated shoulder. By three A.M. the nurses were rotating through their coffee breaks, heading for the cafeteria to grab a soda, a cigarette, a slice of stale pie.

Ellen took the package of raisin cookies down to Mr. Rosen's room. She tiptoed in and left them and a note on his bedside table. For just a second she wished he'd wake up so they could talk, but then she laughed at her own foolishness. What did she want to talk about? A little teasing? A sudden loneliness? Silly! Silently she stepped from his room and hurried to the cafeteria and the company of her friends.

The loud buzz of conversation made her smile. Something was cooking tonight: one of Henry's risqué jokes, or Jeannie's constant parodies of her teenagers' exploits, or Adeline and her gossip. She couldn't wait to join in. But the moment she stepped in the door, silence fell like a bomb.

Ellen stopped for a moment and looked around. Carefully, deliberately, everyone looked away. Then a few heads turned, drawn back to her in curiosity, speculation.

Ellen stood rooted to the spot. Nothing like this had ever happened to her before. These were the people she worked with, her friends; she'd known some of them for years. Now suddenly she felt alien and alone, deserted. Abandoned. She realized her hands were sweating and wiped them on the skirt of her uniform. The movement woke her to action. Something was going on here, and she was damned well going to find out what!

Marching right up to Henry's table, she said, "What is going on here? Are you up to more of your old tricks?"

"Hey, I've got nothing to do with this," he answered, waving his hands in the empty space between them. "Go ask your pal Adeline."

Ellen turned to the next table, but they all were busy staring into their coffee cups. "What is this? Have I got the plague or something? Is my uniform on backward?" No one answered; no one cracked the expected smile. Hurt and bewildered, she looked from one to the other, and finally one girl, a nurse Ellen knew from Elliott Rosen's floor, met her eye. "Come on, Mary, tell me," Ellen said, fighting to maintain her composure.

"Ellen," she said softly, "maybe you'd better take a look at the morning paper."

Ellen's heart slammed against her ribs. Fear rose in a sickening wave inside her, making her mouth taste like rust. "Oh, God . . . no . . ." she whispered, envisioning a car crash, a robbery, some terrible accident and Armand lying hurt somewhere . . . or dead.

Hot tears sprang to her eyes, and her whole body began to shake. "I—I can't," she choked out, her hands hanging like lead weights at her sides. Then panic tore through her body, whipping her into action.

"*Where? What?*" she demanded, her wild eyes flying around the table. "Show me! What's happened?"

Someone stuffed the paper into her hands, and she stared down with wide glazed eyes, but there was nothing . . . nothing.

"Here," came an impatient voice, and the paper was grabbed away, refolded, and shoved back at her. "Here!" A finger tapped at the banner headline on page two: *VSO Conductor Named in Paternity Suit.*

Ellen stared at it a moment. *Oh, thank you, thank you. Oh, dear God, thank you for letting him be all right.* His picture was there, and she touched one finger to his face, feeling her heart start to beat again. She knew she was crying, standing there with the tears streaming down her face, but she couldn't help it.

"Hey, kid, don't take it so hard." Henry sneered. "We all make an ass out of ourselves sometime!"

"Henry, you can really be a jerk," Mary groaned. "I mean, anybody would have fallen for his line. We all saw how slick he was—those flowers, and the way he looks."

"And that limo."

"And that reputation!"

The other women around the table were quick to join in. They were suddenly full of sympathy for Ellen, eager to add their own two cents worth.

"Yeah, Ellen. Any one of us could have made the same mistake."

"I wonder how many other women he's taken advantage of! Doesn't it just make you sick? It says right here that he had promised to marry her and then . . ."

It was as if a fog lifted suddenly from Ellen's brain. The numbness of fear vanished, and she was hearing their words, understanding their meaning.

She jumped back, jerked the paper up, and read the headline again. No, it wasn't possible! Not Armand, not her Armand. "No, it's some mistake—" she said, her voice breaking, and then she ran.

She hid in the locker room, leaning her forehead against the cold metal, waiting for the trembling to stop. When her knees were steady again and she could breathe, she lifted the paper and read the whole article. It took the top third of the page, and it gave dates and quotes. The woman said she had proof: a diary, love letters.

She didn't have any love letters.

Oh, stop it, Farrell! Ellen drew herself up, squared her shoulders, and pushed her hair back into place beneath her cap. She didn't believe a word of this. It was nonsense. It was impossible. She was getting upset over nothing.

Gathering her self-control, she tossed the paper into the trash and headed back out to the E.R.

Adeline fairly jumped across the desk at her. "Oh, Ellen, I hope you haven't seen the morning paper!" A copy was tucked under her arm.

"I've seen it, Adeline."

"Oh, you must be *so* hurt!"

"Nonsense like that can't hurt me, Adeline."

"Oh, I'm so glad," she said, but was obviously annoyed not to have gotten more of a rise out of Ellen. Adeline shrugged then and drifted back to work.

The others stared or looked pointedly elsewhere. There were snickers and laughter and careful silence.

Ellen felt as though she were back in the fifth grade, the only girl to show up the first day of gym class without a training bra.

And not one of these people, these so-called friends, was going to stand by her. The thought made the tears flood her eyes again, and she rubbed them away quickly, hoping no one had seen, but knowing someone had because someone was watching her every minute, waiting to see how she was reacting now. Did she want sympathy? Was she going to fall apart? Was she pale? Did her hands shake? How had the poor thing looked when she heard the news? They'd probably take notes and sell them to the evening edition!

The thought made her sick to her stomach. Suddenly she hurt all over. She wanted to go home, crawl into bed, and hide under the covers. She'd never come out. She had never felt so sick and beaten in her whole life.

"Farrell—phone call." One of the nurses held out the receiver from behind the desk.

Involuntarily Ellen clasped her hands behind her back. Not here, she thought desperately. Not in front of everyone. She just couldn't . . . But then her pride took control. Stubbornly she marched to the desk and held out one hand. It did not shake. "Hello?"

"Ellen? Oh, I'm so glad I got you!"

Recognizing Laurie's voice, Ellen let out her held breath. She swallowed around the tightness in her throat. "Hi, Laurie."

"Ellen, I want you to come right over here after work. Don't go home. Just come right here; there's something—"

"Laurie, I know," she interrupted, keeping her voice even. "I've seen the paper."

"Oh, no! Oh, I wanted you to be here with us. Oh, Rick brought it in while I was nursing the baby, and I—I couldn't stand the thought of you . . . Oh, Ellen, it's got to be a terrible mistake. Someone trying to take advantage of his wealth and fame!"

"Of course."

"Ellen, do you want me to come there? Or Rick? Let Rick come and get you."

"Laurie, I'm fine. I get off in a couple of hours, and then I'm going home. I'll call you later. And thanks, kiddo; I appreciate it."

One more second, one more word, and she'd cry right in front of them all.

She hung up and grabbed the chart of the next patient. "Mr. Rodriguez? We're going to take you upstairs for X rays. First I need a little information."

She kept busy, determined to get through those next two hours with her pride intact. It wasn't easy. The moment she let down her guard, the pain struck like a knife twisting in her heart. The memory of Armand on the beach, outlined against sand and sea, or in bed, his dark head on the pillow, made her want to weep. His voice whispered in her head, saying, "I love you. It's all right, trust me."

Oh, God, please don't let me cry here.

At 6:55 she dropped the chart she was holding back into its slot and walked into the locker room. Promptly at 7:00 she pulled on her jacket and clocked out.

Armand was waiting just inside the front door of the hospital, watching for her. His jacket was unbuttoned, his hands thrust into the pockets of his slacks. His dark hair was windblown. His face was ashen, and against the sudden pallor of his skin his eyes seemed to burn like coals. "Ellen," he called when he saw her. He said nothing but her name, his voice even and empty.

Ellen nodded and went to him, walking without hurrying across the E.R., her head up, her shoulders back like a soldier. She slipped her hand through his arm and they left. Neither spoke till they were out on the street in front of the playground. Then Armand said, "So. You've seen it." His voice seemed to come from some empty place within him.

She looked up at his profile and saw the muscles jump in his cheek. The angle of his jaw was as sharp as a knife blade. Hard. Angry. Hurt.

"Yes," she answered. "They deliver the paper to

the hospital early, and everyone made sure I got a copy."

He turned to her, cupping her face in his hands, his eyes blazing with pain. "Oh, Lord, I am sorry, Ellen! I didn't want you to have to see that alone."

"Oh, I wasn't alone. There were lots of my"—she paused, the words tasting bitter—"my friends around." She struggled against tears. "Some of them were glad it happened. I could tell. It was like they thought I deserved it for . . . for wanting too much, getting too much. For showing off."

"You could *never* do that! Oh, *cara*, you are the gentlest, most loving—" He wiped her tears away with his hands. "Don't cry. Forget them! That's not even what I meant. I didn't want you to have to go through this without me there with you. *I* am your friend. Your friend and lover. And I want to be your husband."

Ellen closed her eyes, but the tears slid out between her lashes and rolled to the corners of her mouth. She couldn't answer. There were no words in her, no thoughts or feelings, just this terrible pain. Why, oh, why, had he brought marriage up now?

His hands tightened on her shoulders. "Look at me, Ellen. Please, just look in my eyes."

But she couldn't.

He spun away and she heard the slam of his fist into the chain link fence lining the playground. There was a kick that rattled the chain, and then another slam of his hands against the metal.

"Stop! Don't—you'll hurt your hands."

"My hands? What the hell do I care about my hands?"

"They're your life."

"No! *You're* my life. Everything else I'd give up, throw away. I don't want any of it if it can hurt you like this."

"I'm okay, Armand," she said quickly, frightened by the rash look in his eyes.

"Are you? Then stop looking like someone's put a knife in your heart and is twisting it."

"I'm fine." She forced a tiny smile. "Really. You're the emotional one. It's all that performing, all that drama up at the podium. You get too excited about things. I'm calm now. I'm okay."

Eyes narrowed, he watched her, his dark gaze burning her face. He tipped his head forward, and his hair spilled over one brow. His lips were edged white with tension. "Are you? Good." His chest rose and fell with his ragged breaths. "Good, then you know this is just a mistake. A sick attempt at publicity-seeking."

"But who would *do* that, Armand?"

"Lots of people would. Heaven knows why, but they think someone like me is public property." A muscle jumped at the corner of his mouth. "Ellen, I can't explain why this is happening. I can only tell you that I love you, and you have to trust me."

"But you must know this woman. She says she has pictures, letters. . . ." She stepped back, her voice trailing off to a whisper. Across the space between them her gaze was trusting but terribly frightened.

Armand reached out and touched her hair. He wanted to do more—hold her, kiss away her sadness, banish her doubts—but he knew she would not let him do that now. Not now . . . and perhaps not ever again. The thought struck him like a physical blow. Sickened, he staggered and dropped his hand to her narrow shoulder to steady himself.

He felt her stiffen. Was she drawing away already, holding herself apart from him? That same uncompromising honesty of hers that he loved could condemn them to a life apart!

He would lose her.

Oh, Lord, he would die without her! He had to convince her, prove there was nothing to be afraid of. Fighting to keep his voice calm, he said, "Ellen, she and I knew each other before I ever met you."

"Was that in the biblical sense, Armand?" she asked with an attempt at a smile, but her blue eyes glistened with tears.

He drew a breath. "Yes. But it was"—his eyes flicked away and back again—"it was very casual. She made it quite clear that I was not the only man she was seeing. She wanted to make quite sure I understood that I was not *that* special."

"Then this *could* be your child."

"It is not my child!"

"But Armand, if it is . . ."

"It is not! I haven't seen that woman for months and months, not since you came into my life. Why, *why* would I ever have wanted to see anyone once I saw you?"

His voice broke and he raked a bruised hand through his dark hair. "Ellen, she was the one you saw coming out of my building the other day. She came to me angry, jealous, desperate. She said she wanted us to pick up the relationship again. I told her . . . I told her there had *been* no relationship, that we had both had a good time but it was over. I told her I was in love with you. She—she said I'd be sorry, that she was used to getting what she wanted, no matter how! And then she stormed out and almost ran you over." His voice was suddenly fierce. "Ellen, she never even mentioned a word about being pregnant."

"Maybe it was too terrible for her," Ellen whispered, crying again. "Maybe she was too embarrassed, or frightened—"

"Maybe she knew it was not mine!"

"But still—"

"But *what*? Why do you argue for *her*? Take *my* side. Trust me! I tell you, that child is not mine!"

She hung her head, suddenly weary to the bone. She wanted to go to sleep, to hide in her bed and not think, not talk, just forget all about this. It was too much, too foreign and strange. Nothing in her life had prepared her for this.

"Armand. . . ." She wiped a trembling hand across her brow. "I don't know, maybe you could take that blood test. Prove it isn't you and then the papers will print a retraction and—"

"Never!" He stiffened, his brow black as thunder. "Don't you see, that's just what they want. They could fill whole columns with interviews with the doctors, pictures of me going to the hospital, expert testimony on whether the test is valid or not. Oh, *she'd* love it! Her lawyer would contact my lawyer to discuss an out-of-court settlement to spare us both further anguish. . . . Never!"

Armand took hold of her shoulders, the grip of his hands powerful, commanding. But his voice was soft and gentle. "Ellen, listen to me."

She put the flat of her hand against his chest, touching him, but holding him at bay. "Armand, I don't want to listen. I need to go home. I need time to think."

"No, I don't want you to think! I don't want to give you time to be cool and rational. I don't want you to weigh the consequences, consider the future. Ellen, I never told you loving me would be easy. I never said that! It won't be, not if I am famous, a celebrity, 'the great Dante, our illustrious conductor'! But"—he brushed her hand away, pulling her tight against the hard wall of his chest, his words muffled in her hair—"but I don't have to be a celebrity. I can give that up. I can do something else!"

"Oh, Armand, don't be silly!"

"There you go again." He laughed softly against her cheek. "Oh, my dearest, my darling—"

"No, Armand, I'm serious now! What do you think you would do? Take a job in an office somewhere? Give music lessons to little children in your spare time?"

"I could compose. We could buy that home way out on the beach and I could write my music."

"And hear someone else conduct it, never being the one to lift that music up from the orchestra to the very roof of the concert hall? Oh, Armand, I've watched you when the music flows through you; it's your life. Taking that away would be like cutting off your hands."

"Losing you would be like cutting out my heart!"

She brushed the hair away from his eyes. "Oh, Armand, you are a hopeless romantic. You and your dear grand gestures. But you're wrong. You couldn't be anyone but who you are, and . . . and if you tried, you'd grow to hate yourself, and me!"

"Hate you? Never! *Ellen, I love you.*"

"And I love you."

"Then nothing else matters! Not the publicity, not the lies, not the scandal or gossip columns."

"But they do! They *do* matter, even if I don't want them to." Hot tears were scalding her cheeks again, staining the front of his shirt. "Even if I lied and said I could live with the scandal, pretend not to hear, it would hurt me."

"I won't let it. I'll find a way not to let it touch you! I will!"

"Armand, no one can promise that. You can't fight the whole world. You can't *change* the whole world! No one can, not even you."

"I will if that's what it takes to make you mine. Oh, Ellen, I have never loved anyone before and I will never love anyone again. No one but you. Only you."

"Armand," she said, swallowing her tears, tilting her chin up to look right into his dark eyes. "Don't be silly. There's always someone else you can love. Someone else at another time and place. Someone in the future."

"Is there?" Wrapping his arms more tightly around her, he pressed his mouth into her hair. "Is there, Ellen? Is there someone else for you?"

"There may have to be," she whispered stubbornly. "I—I may have made a mistake. I'm not like you. I can't look past the gossip, ignore it. It embarrasses me. I know how I felt when I saw that paper. I think of having to tell my parents, or worse, of someone else telling them. I think of having children, and having them see something like that, and I want to die. I can't do this. I can't live like this. I was wrong. I loved you so much, I thought I could do anything; I thought nothing else mattered. But things do matter."

"Nothing matters but us!" The words seemed torn from Armand's throat. He looked down at her, his dark eyes full of love, full of torment.

"I wish I believed that," she cried, his beloved face a blur through her tears, "but I don't!" And tearing herself free of his arms, she ran blindly toward her car.

Ten

Ellen tried to push the front door of her apartment building open with her shoulder. She felt too tired even to raise her hands. She leaned her forehead against the cool glass and closed her eyes, wishing some magic force would carry her through the lobby and up into her own safe, dark apartment. A sharp tap on the other side of the glass made her jump.

"Ms. Farrell?" Clarence pulled the door open and stood aside. "Come on in. Are you all right?"

"I'm fine, Clarence."

"Hey, you can't fool me! Ms. Farrell, if I'm not out of line, I just want to tell you, I read the paper and I wouldn't waste a minute's sleep on stuff like that. I'm a good judge of character, and that man of yours is okay. Just forget this crazy stuff."

"Clarence, thanks. Really. But I don't want to talk about it."

"Okay, sure, but just one more thing. I played

cards with him, right, and I can tell you he didn't cheat. I know, because I do! Naw, your guy's okay; you can trust him."

"Thank you, Clarence," she said, her throat tight with tears.

"Think nothin' of it. Hey, if any reporters come by, should I say you're not home?"

Her apartment was blessedly quiet, dark, and shadowed by the drawn curtains. Ellen pulled off her jacket, unbuttoned her uniform, and started to hang her clothes away. Suddenly she was sobbing right out loud, her mouth open and her face wet and crumpled. She stood there in front of the closet, crying like a little girl, with a child's hopelessness. Her heart was broken. She couldn't move, couldn't stop, couldn't do anything but let her sobs shake her. Oh, what was she going to do now? For the first time, she wished she had never left the convent. She wished she were locked away, safe, silent, where nothing could touch her, where she'd never want anything, never have anything. . . .

The jangle of the phone was like a hot coal pressed to her skin. She jumped back, almost knocking over a lamp, and stood frozen, her hands covering her mouth. "Stop," she wept, "oh, stop; go away; leave me alone."

Finally the phone stopped ringing, and her sobs died to hiccups. Pressing her hand to her aching chest, she staggered to the bed and hid her face in her pillow. Why? Why did this have to happen? It just wasn't fair. She'd spent so many years being strong, independent. Helping others. Weathering crisis after crisis. How could this happen to her?

A wave of self-loathing washed over her, knocking the breath right out of her lungs. Oh, *she* was the cheat! *She* was the liar. She wasn't strong at all! She was scared, scared to death of seeing her name in the paper and wondering what people thought, or, worse, *knowing* what they thought and that they were laughing at her. She couldn't stand that; she couldn't go through an experience like this morning again. No! She'd find a safe, protected way to live . . . a quiet, safe place where nothing could hurt her . . . a dark, safe place. . . .

Like a child, she lulled herself to sleep with promises.

She woke later, feeling numb. She wouldn't look at the clock; she kept her face turned away from the window as the slanting late afternoon light deepened to dusk. The birds sang outside her window, but she wouldn't listen to them. The wind picked up, rattling the windowpanes with a hint of the winter to come, but she never heard it. She just lay there, trying not to think or feel anything.

When the phone rang, she jumped and waited for her heart to slow. Lifting the receiver took great effort, as if it were made of lead.

"Hello?"

"Ellen, it's Rick. Laurie and I were worried about you; you didn't call."

"I took a nap." She sighed, trying to think of something perky and reassuring to say, but she was just too tired. "I'm okay."

"Well, you sound rotten, but you've just got to hang in there. Be tough! How's Armand?"

"I . . ." She covered her eyes with her hand. "I don't know."

"Ellen—"

She could hear the mixture of concern and disapproval in Rick's voice. "Rick, I'm really exhausted. I'll talk to you later."

"Ellen, you've got to realize this is just one of those lousy things that can happen when you're a celebrity! You've got to trust him! You've got to—"

"I don't have to do anything but climb back into bed!"

"Well, before you run and hide, maybe you'd better take a look at the evening paper."

"Dammit, don't you think I've had enough of papers for one day!" she shouted, her voice breaking.

"I know," he said softly. "I know this must be terrible for you. But we're with you, kiddo. We love you. And if you love him, you'll get through this."

"Rick, I'm hanging up!"

"Just take a look at the gossip column, Ellen," he concluded before she hung up.

She sat in the shadows, staring at the locked door as if an enemy waited just on the other side. The room grew dark. She tried not to think, not to feel anything, but, like feathers shaken from a pillow, tiny memories began to whirl behind her eyes: Armand laughing, the wind whipping his dark hair, the angle of his brow, the shadow of beard on his jaw in the morning before he shaved, the flash of his hand holding the baton on a downbeat, the crinkly sound his dress shirt made when he pulled it free of his black pants and pressed her against his bare chest, the dizzying scent of his cologne. . . .

She started to cry again, harsh, rasping sobs of grief.

Oh, she couldn't bear it, not one way or the other. How could she live his life? But how could she live without him?

Armand. . . .

She reached for the phone and dialed his number, but there was no answer. Where would he be? Whom would he have turned to, that proud and stubborn man? Did he have a Rick or Laurie to call and comfort him?

The thought brought Rick's words hurtling back to her: *the paper.* What now? What more could happen?

The evening edition had been delivered to her door, and she tore through it, sending sheets of newsprint flying through the room until she found the gossip column. There it was, salt for the wound:

> Guess what we overheard at an intimate luncheon at the Villa Capri. Those in the know were speculating on the menu for this year's Autumn-in-Virginia Brunch for the V.S.O.:
> > Vichyssoise
> > Salade Mimosa
> > Armand Dante's Cooked Goose
> What we want to know, Maestro, is who will be doing the carving?

Anger finally washed away her self-pity, her fear, everything but her love.

How dare they? How dare they make fun of that glorious, wonderful man? They, who applauded his music, who stood and screamed "Bravo," threw roses on the stage, and waited outside the concert hall for pictures and autographs, who pulled on his sleeve, and tried to snip off locks of his hair. They wrote letters that embarrassed him and sent gifts he'd never accept. They wanted everything: his music, his talent, his time, a scrap of his attention. Given it, they'd throw themselves at his feet, or in his arms if he'd let them! And here they were, smiling their smug smiles. . . .

Oh, she'd like to make them eat every word!

But how?

She caught the loose ends of her hair and wrapped and unwrapped them around her fingers the way she used to when she was a little girl. *Think, Farrell.* She marched around the room, tugging at her hair. She'd made an awful mess of today. She'd run and hidden when she should have stood her ground. She'd left Armand to face trouble all alone when she should have wrapped him in her love. If this was a test of her courage, she'd gotten a big, fat F. But . . . if she had another chance, she planned on getting nothing but A+'s from now until eternity!

Armand . . . Armand would know what to do now. She dialed his number again, her heart racing; she could feel the beat of her pulse at her wrist and temple. The phone rang and rang, but still there was no answer. Where could he be? She chewed at her lip in frustration, tugged at her hair, and then stopped stock-still in the middle of the room.

The concert hall! He had a performance tonight. But no! He couldn't have gone to stand there alone at the podium and face the mockery and derision, the prying, judging eyes of the crowd.

She pressed the heels of both hands to her eyes, making lights burst inside her head. She knew that was just what he had done. She could see him now, dark head held high, his shoulders braced, black eyes flashing in his pale face. Brave and unbending, he'd give them their music and nothing else.

Checking her watch, she saw she could just make it if she hurried. She stormed through the apartment, turning on every light and throwing the windows open to the cool night air. In a flurry of activity she showered, put on some makeup, and slipped into a dress Armand had admired whenever she wore it, a soft red wool that he said woke the fire sleeping in her hair and skin. One shoe on, the other still in her hand, she hopped to the door and pulled it open just in time to hear the pounding of a man's footsteps racing up the three flights of stairs.

"Armand?" she called in surprise.

"No, it's me, Rick! Laurie's in the car with the baby."

Ellen raced down to meet him. "Wonderful! All troops assembled and ready to do battle!"

"You bet!" He grinned, giving her a good hard bear hug. "That's the Ellen we know and love. Now, where to?"

"The concert hall. And hurry!"

They arrived just minutes before the concert was to start.

"Do you want us to come in with you?" Rick asked.

"No, I think I'll do this myself. But thank you, all three of you!"

"No need to thank us," Laurie answered with a hug. "And we'll be back to pick you up. Don't argue; it'll be a lot safer that way! Now, go give 'em hell!"

Ellen ran to the ticket window. "One seat please, Jane," she said to the tall thin woman in the ticket booth whom she had gotten to know during her frequent visits to the concert hall.

"Oh! Ms. Farrell, I didn't expect—"

"Jane, I'm in a hurry!"

"Sure! You just go on in! The maestro will be glad to see you!" And she flashed a sudden bright smile.

Ellen nodded quickly at the usherette standing at the top of the aisle, and the woman's brows jumped into her gray bangs. "I'm going to sit up front, Doris. Thank you."

And then she paced her steps, walking proudly, solemnly, down the long, carpeted aisle, her head held high, her clear blue gaze fastened on the empty stage ahead.

Heads turned. A few people recognized her, some from her constant attendance at Armand's concerts, and others from the picture that had appeared in the paper. Whispers spread like a chill breeze, causing heads to nod like so many flowers on slender stems. Ellen ignored them all. She had wrapped herself in courage and love, and nothing could touch her.

When she was but a few rows from the front, the lights dimmed. A small patter of nervous applause rose from the audience, and Armand Dante strode out of the wings and into the spotlight.

She'd never seen him look more handsome. His

skin had the pale glow of polished marble, perfect and bloodless, and his fierce dark eyes shone against it. His back was straight, his shoulders squared, as if his body had been molded to face adversity. He radiated such a spirit of valor and defiance that Ellen stopped in her tracks, breathless.

Armand reached the podium, bowed to his orchestra, and then turned to face the hostile audience.

What he saw was Ellen.

Their eyes locked and held. It was like a physical touch, the love was so strong between them. Her upturned face was suddenly wet with tears, but she was smiling. Armand took one step forward, bowed to her, and drew his first easy breath of the day.

It was so silent in that vast hall that Ellen could hear the hiss of his breath through his teeth. She could hear the thumping of her heart. The audience was held spellbound, and remained absolutely silent as Armand turned back to the orchestra, lifted his baton, and woke the music to life.

Hours later, when he brought it to its glorious finale, the hall again fell into a strange, unearthly silence. And then Ellen leaped to her feet, rapt with the pleasure of his performance. "Bravo!" she shouted, applauding wildly. "Bravo!" Her one thin voice echoed through the hall.

And then the entire audience rose to its feet, cheering and applauding, saluting the man standing alone at the podium. The orchestra rose behind him en masse, their applause adding to the swell of approbation that shook the roof.

Armand let his dark gaze sweep the hall, his eyes shining, and then he bowed once and left the stage.

Ellen dashed to the wings.

"Armand?" she whispered, afraid to trust her voice.

"Ellen! Oh, love—"

He caught her in his arms, holding her close and burying his face in her hair. "Ellen," he whispered again, his voice hoarse and full of unspoken emotion.

She slipped her arms beneath his jacket, wanting to hold him, protect him, wrap him in her love. She could feel how his shirt clung damply to his back and chest. She felt the heat of him, the pounding of his heart, the harsh intake of his breath.

"Are you all right?" she breathed, pressing her lips to the pulse beating in his throat.

"I don't know yet," he answered gravely as he swept her up in his arms and carried her down the hall to his dressing room.

Inside, he kicked the door shut, put her down, and then leaned over her, his hands pressed to the wall behind her head, his face inches away. She could see the dark shadows beneath his eyes and the lines of tension etched across his brow.

She reached up and tried to smooth the pain away. "Oh, darling, was it terrible?"

"Not too bad. They can't hurt me. Only you can do that."

"Armand." His soul was in his eyes, and the love she saw there calmed her, giving her all the strength she'd ever need. She reached up and touched his face. "Forgive me, love."

"Ellen, there's nothing to forgive. I asked too much. I was being stubborn, proud, but I'll take that blood test and force a retraction—"

"No! You have nothing to prove. And it's because you are stubborn and proud and brave and glorious that I love you." The tears rolled down her cheeks, but she didn't even try to stop them. "Armand, I love you."

"I never doubted that, my beauty," he whispered. "But you are right, I can't promise anything." His voice broke, but he went on, fierce with determination. "Believe me, I want to, Ellen. I want to promise that nothing like this will ever happen again, that I can keep the world at bay, that I can stop it from ever touching us."

"It's all right," she insisted, gently tracing one dark brow with her finger.

"No, it isn't! But I can stand it. The joy of the music, my work, they're my reward. But you—"

"*You* are *my* reward. And I'm stronger than you think!" she said tenderly, her blue eyes shining with love. "I'm stronger than *I* thought. I learned that today, after I stopped running and hiding. The only thing I'm sorry about"—she sniffed back the tears that threatened—"the only thing I regret is that I didn't realize it this morning. But you were *something* up at that podium tonight! Indomitable!"

A grin tugged at the corner of his beautiful mouth. "The columns will probably picture me as cold and heartless."

"Let them! I know better," she whispered, sliding her hands down his shoulders and letting them come to rest against his chest. "There's my proof!"

And she bent her head and pressed her lips to the starched front of his shirt just over his heart.

Armand closed his eyes for a second; her sweet form had gone all blurry suddenly. Then he bowed his dark head and kissed the top of her hair. "Ellen." His voice was a husky murmur almost lost in the warm chestnut tangle. "I love you. There is no one in the world for me but you. You *are* my world!"

Ellen thought her heart would surely fly out of her breast like some caged bird set free. Then she laughed, a rich, ripe sound full of happiness. "Okay, Maestro, come on and prove it!"

She felt him stiffen involuntarily, passion tightening his muscles like a jolt of lightning. Then he lifted her up against his body, kissing her, holding her, reassuring himself that she was real, was his forever.

Ellen parted her lips to accept his kiss and all the promise it held. She was going to share her life with this glorious, wonderful man. How had she ever gotten so lucky? The answer was in his eyes and his smile and his touch.

Reaching up, she began to undo his bow tie, unbutton his shirt, and then gasped, shaken by a sudden burst of laughter.

"I don't believe it! I forgot Rick and Laurie are waiting outside with the baby. They're our armed escort home."

"Who? What!"

Armand leaned one shoulder against the doorframe, toying with a strand of her hair. His face softened into pleased bemusement. "I should have known. You, love, you and your friends; when you take someone into your heart, he or she is safe there forever." He swallowed, nodding. "Do you know, Clarence called earlier and left a strange message, that he had a bottle of champagne and a deck of cards waiting for my next visit!"

"Oh, Armand." She laughed, happier than she ever thought she could be. "I love you."

"And I love you." He opened the door and had just stepped out into the hall when the phone inside the dressing room rang.

They exchanged a wordless glance, and then Armand reached for the phone. He listened for a moment and then smiled. "Yes, sir, we're here together; everything will be all right. And thank you for the call."

He held the receiver out to her. "Ellen?"

"Hello?" she said warily, then sighed and smiled. "Yes, Dad, we're fine. Can you believe that ridiculous story? I guess it's going to take a little practice, being a symphony conductor's wife."

With a whoop of joy Armand wrapped her in his arms and kissed her as if he would never stop.

Epilogue

Readers, have we got a scoop for you:

Not only was this column the first to print the retraction of that ridiculous story concerning VSO Conductor Armand Dante (not that we believed it for one moment!), but we have just received news that Maestro Dante, the darling of local society, has married! Maestro, shame on you for keeping such a thrilling secret from us, your loyal fans. We send our best wishes to you and your beautiful bride. And we are looking forward to another exciting and eventful symphony season.

(And, to whoever was kind enough to send us this lovely picture of the bride and groom honeymooning in Italy, thank you so much!)

"You're welcome!" Laurie laughed, and went to feed the baby.

THE EDITOR'S CORNER

If there were a theme for next month's LOVESWEPT romances, it might be "Pennies from Heaven," because in all four books something wonderful seems to drop from above right into the lives of our heroes or heroines.

First, in Peggy Webb's utterly charming **DONOVAN'S ANGEL**, LOVESWEPT #143, Martie Fleming tumbles down (literally) into Paul Donovan's garden. Immediately fascinated by Martie, Paul feels she is indeed a blessing straight from heaven—an especially appropriate notion as he's a minister. But, discovering his vocation, Martie runs for cover, convinced that she is so unconventional she could never be a clergyman's wife. Most of the parishioners seem to agree: her spicy wit and way-out clothes and unusual occupation set their tongues wagging. Paul, determined as he is to have Martie, seems fated to lose . . . until a small miracle or two intervenes. You simply can't let yourself miss this funny, heartwarming love story that so perfectly captures the atmosphere of a small Southern town.

The very title of our next romance, **WILD BLUE YONDER**, LOVESWEPT #144, by Millie Grey, gives you a clue to how it fits our theme. Mike Donahue pilots an antique biplane like a barnstormer of years gone by. And when he develops engine trouble and lands on Krissa Colbrook's property, he's soon devel-

(continued)

oping trouble for her too . . . trouble of the heart. The last kind of man placid Krissa needs or wants in her life is a daredevil, yet she falls hard for this irresistible vagabond who's come to her from the sky above. We think it would be hard for a reader to fail to be charmed by Mike, so we feel secure in saying that you will be enchanted by the way Mike goes about ridding Krissa of her fears!

For just a second now try to put yourself into the very large shoes of one Morgan Abbott, hero of talented newcomer Linda Cajio's **ALL IS FAIR . . .**, LOVESWEPT #145. Imagine that you (you're that handsome Morgan, remember?) are having dinner with acquaintances when an absolutely stunning beauty—who is also a perfect stranger—rushes up and kisses you passionately before quickly disappearing. Then, another day in another city, the same gorgeous lady again appears suddenly, kisses you senseless and vanishes. Wouldn't your head be reeling? Well, those are just two of the several unique ways that Cecilia St. Martin gets to Abbott. You will relish this wildly wonderful, very touching romance from Linda who makes her truly stylish, truly nifty debut as a romance writer with us.

And last, but never, never least is the beautiful romance **JOURNEY'S END**, LOVESWEPT #146, by Joan Elliott Pickart. In this dramatic and tender love story Victoria Blair finds everything she ever dreamed of having in the arms of Sage Lawson, owner of the Lazy L ranch just outside Sunshine, New Mexico. Indeed at times sunshine does seem to pour down on these two lovely people who appear to be made in heaven for each other. Yet ominous clouds of doubt and misunderstanding threaten their budding love. Sage

(continued)

grows hostile, Blair becomes distant, withdrawn. Clearly they need a little push back into one another's arms . . . and the matchmakers and the ways they give that little push are sure to delight you.

As always, we hope that each of these four LOVE-SWEPTs will give you the greatest of pleasure.

With warm good wishes,

Carolyn Nichols

Carolyn Nichols
  Editor
LOVESWEPT
Bantam Books, Inc.
666 Fifth Avenue
New York, NY 10103

LOVESWEPT

Love Stories you'll never forget by authors you'll always remember

☐	21657	**The Greatest Show on Earth #47** Nancy Holder	$2.25
☐	21658	**Beware the Wizard #48** Sara Orwig	$2.25
☐	21660	**The Man Next Door #49** Kathleen Downes	$2.25
☐	21633	**In Search of Joy #50** Noelle Berry McCue	$2.25
☐	21659	**Send No Flowers #51** Sandra Brown	$2.25
☐	21652	**Casey's Cavalier #52** Olivia & Ken Harper	$2.25
☐	21654	**Little Consequences #53** Barbara Boswell	$2.25
☐	21653	**The Gypsy & the Yachtsman #54** Joan J. Domning	$2.25
☐	21664	**Capture the Rainbow #55** Iris Johansen	$2.25
☐	21662	**Encore #56** Kimberly Wagner	$2.25
☐	21640	**Unexpected Sunrise #57** Helen Mittermeyer	$2.25
☐	21665	**Touch the Horizon #59** Iris Johansen	$2.25

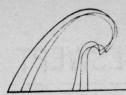 # LOVESWEPT

Love Stories you'll never forget by authors you'll always remember

☐ 21708	**Out of This World #103**	Nancy Holder	$2.25
☐ 21699	**Rachel's Confession #107**	Fayrene Preston	$2.25
☐ 21716	**A Tough Act to Follow #108**	Billie Green	$2.25
☐ 21718	**Come As You Are #109**	Laurien Berenson	$2.25
☐ 21719	**Sunlight's Promise #110**	Joan Elliott Pickart	$2.25
☐ 21726	**Dear Mitt #111**	Sara Orwig	$2.25
☐ 21729	**Birds Of A Feather #112**	Peggy Web	$2.25
☐ 21727	**A Matter of Magic #113**	Linda Hampton	$2.25
☐ 21728	**Rainbow's Angel #114**	Joan Elliott Pickart	$2.25

Prices and availability subject to change without notice.

Buy them at your local bookstore or use this handy coupon for ordering:

Bantam Books, Inc., Dept. SW2, 414 East Golf Road, Des Plaines, Ill. 60016

Please send me the books I have checked above. I am enclosing $_____
(please add $1.50 to cover postage and handling). Send check or money
—no cash or C.O.D.'s please.

Mr/Mrs/Miss_____

Address_____

City_____State/Zip_____

SW2—4/86

Please allow four to six weeks for delivery. This offer expires 10/86.

Special Offer
Buy a Bantam Book
for only 50¢.

Now you can have an up-to-date listing of Bantam's hundreds of titles plus take advantage of our unique and exciting bonus book offer. A special offer which gives you the opportunity to purchase a Bantam book for only 50¢. Here's how!

By ordering any five books at the regular price per order, you can also choose any other single book listed (up to a $4.95 value) for just 50¢. Some restrictions do apply, but for further details why not send for Bantam's listing of titles today!

Just send us your name and address and we will send you a catalog!

LOVESWEPT

Love Stories you'll never forget by authors you'll always remember